Filmic Cuts 2

Luchador Monkey Crisis

Filmic Cuts V.2
Luchador Monkey Crisis

Short Stories by

Oli Jacobs

For Sam, my brother from another mother, occasional saviour, and sobering Ying to my raging Yang

Contents

Foreword by Michael Williams

Checkmate

Happy As Larry

Nought To Sixty

In The Room With Rosie

The Bird Cage

Sense (III & IV)

The Legend of the Rogue

Sanctuary

*feedthetroll

Ringside with the Kid

The Dead Men

Foreword

Every man and woman walking upon this Earth has a talent – a skill. Some may keep what it is to themselves, whilst others may have talents that couldn't be bought up in general conversation; Badger Baiting for example. Oli Jacobs does not have just one talent. He is a swiss army knife of a man.

I first met Oli in September 2012 at a geeky social gathering. Being a friend of a friend, I spent that evening in his company and he endeared himself to me faster than anyone else. He was jovial, he cracked good jokes and most importantly, he had a bountiful beard. So after that evening I did the thing we all do, and added those we met on Facebook and Twitter. Me and Oli chatted, found common ground, and about six weeks later I had left my writing post on one website and jumped ship to the site that Oli co-managed.

I knew Oli was a writer before he even mentioned the fact, my brain sort of acts like a gaydar for literate beings. There's a huge difference between 'being a writer' and being a writer like Oli Jacobs, though. I've been told in the past that I have a drive to get to where I want with my own career. To that I say nay and can use Oli as a perfect example. Each evening I can glance over my Twitter feed and see Oli working for hours on end on his latest prose. Oli has that unprecedented drive to do what he wants and get to where he wants to be. He also has that skillset and immense style to turn each tale into a linguistic treat. The proudest moment was filming Oli do a presentation at High Wycombe library on self-publishing. Why? Because it was easy to see, that even through the nerves, Oli was delivering his raucous style and getting people involved on his level – he was sharing his drive with a room packed full of people. He was bringing strangers into the OJ way of life.

In your hands is Filmic Cuts Volume 2 – a Chinese buffet of a book. When you dine at a Chinese buffet, you want to mix it up. Have a searing hot heap of duck, but then still have enough room for some potato Smilies. Or is it just Chinese buffets in Wolverhampton that put out of place McCains foodstuffs out. Either way, my point is that just like the original Filmic Cuts, you have been presented with a book full of tales with different pacing and tones, ready to keep you coming back for more.

More you shall always have with Oli, for his is a mind that will constantly come up with fresh ideas, building into a list that will one day fill a library – a library that won't need to sustain itself by sellotaping a Costa on top of it. Oli isn't just a writer. He is a maverick, an amazing freestyle comedian and most importantly to me, one of my best friends who has been there to listen and help me with both projects and life in general. If you ever meet Oli then you will have that same connection moment I had. Oli is a great man and by letting him into your life by way of this book, you too shall soon be touched.

Not like that. Well, maybe if you buy ten copies of Bad Sandwich.

Michael Williams (aka Micster) is the Deputy Editor of gaming website Nerfed.co.uk, where he writes witty stuff about video games. He is also the much-heralded director of short films Paper Jam, Echo, *and* Nilin Remembers, *through Laughing Duck Productions. Follow him on Twitter as @_micster or visit his website www.micster.com. He has donated his fee back to the author.*

Checkmate

Within the stark white walls of their prison, time was a relative concept for the two men. How long they slept? They couldn't tell you. When they ate? Again a mystery. The only sign of any passage of time were the wrinkles on their skin and the follicle growth that sprouted from their heads and face. Everything else was just still.

They had been there a while though, they knew that. Again there was a vague quality to what that consisted of, the last calendar they had acquired lost all meaning 3 months in when an argument arose as to whether it was one day or another. That had been the first sign of madness between them, and thankfully the last. Both men were self-aware enough that should this isolation take them, it would kill them. They needed to stay focused, keep busy. Thankfully there was plenty to occupy them. Papers, art materials... they had created masterpieces in their own eyes several times over, but what really kept them from collapsing was the chess set.

The Older Man, more haggard than the Younger but blessed with years of knowledge that his advanced years gave him, set up the board. It was one of those 'Learn to...' ones, with faded instructions on the board showing where each piece was allowed to move to. Of course to both men this was now an irrelevance, while they were no Grand Masters they knew each other enough to produce a fierce game. The pieces were delicately and methodically placed upon the board, stood proudly upon their starting places before the heat of battle would call them into action. The line of pawns, ready to sacrifice themselves toward the greater good, the Knights dancing around the board in an unpredictable manner and of course, the King and Queen standing waiting.

The Younger Man approached when the board was set up and looked over it. He didn't say anything, he didn't have to, instead just taking his seat and stretching his back ready to work his mental muscles. As per their age-old agreement, he was Yellow (the Learn to...'s equivalent of White) while his elder took the Black.

"Here we go again," the Younger quipped, drawing a smile from his compatriot. "After you."

"I thought you won the last?"

The Younger Man merely shrugged. If he was honest he had lost count of the Win-Loss record between them, but he again obliged with a gesture of his hand.

"Very well," said The Elder, and moved the first piece.

Pawn to E4

In silence, The Younger Man had his response without even thinking. It was systematic by now, an opening salvo by both men that would mean nothing in the grander scheme of things. They both knew how this game was played, and were eager to get to the interesting bits. Everything that preceded it was just useless foreplay.

Pawn to E5

"Feeling OK?" The Younger Man asked, looking across the table at the Elder.

The Elder didn't respond at first, instead concentrating on the board. In his mind he laughed, knowing this sort of emotional power play was typical of the Younger Man.

Knight to F3

"The usual. Tired, bored, depressed."

"Even with my fine company?"

The Elder gave another light smile. He had always enjoyed the Younger Man's wit and humour. Even as they toiled through dark and hard days, the Younger Man had always managed to come forward with a pun or a crack. They had known each other long before the events that had occurred. The Elder had watched as, at first, the Younger Man had struggled with the situation, and he had to become a calming influence. But now the person he knew had returned, at least partly anyway. There was still a subtle sadness to him.

Knight to C6

The Elder looked over at his opponent, and saw that maudlin streak bubbling under the surface. Something was definitely troubling him this time around, but he had found it was best to wait until the Younger Man broached the subject himself. He made his move silently, in both the physical and mental game.

Knight to C3

The Younger Man shifted in his seat a little, and looked down at the board. The untrained eye would say that he was analysing his options, trying to look one, two, maybe three moves ahead. But the Elder knew differently, the frantic pace to which the Younger Man's eyes darted in their sockets meant there was more than chess going on behind the scenes. He didn't have to wait any longer as the Younger Man made his move.

Knight to F6

"So..." he began, briefly looking up to the Elder for a response. The Elder didn't respond straight away, instead choosing to move.

Pawn to A3

"So?" he responded calmly, finally meeting the Younger Man's gaze. He was definitely troubled, as the ready smile had faded and left a fallen, heavy expression. The Younger Man was ready to talk, but instead swiftly placed his move on the board.

Pawn to D5

"How much longer do you think we have?" he asked the Elder, as quickly as his hand had moved his piece. The Elder noticed how the Younger Man began to rub his hands together, a sign that he was agitated or concerned. After they had arrived it was revealed to him that the Younger Man had a condition that caused involuntary tics and spasms, and while they were rarely violent enough to cause concern, they were usually preceded by this hand-wringing.

The Elder knew the best course of action was to calm him down. There was no need to bring up any stress or anything else that would plant negativity within the Younger Man. After all, the scenario itself was far too big to worry about the little things. Age had taught him that.

He rubbed his long, grey-speckled beard and turned his eyes to the board. There was an opportunity there for him, but the question was as to whether it was a trap or a genuine mistake by his opponent. Equally, this line of questioning, a loaded, potentially dark conversation topic, could also be seen as both frailty on the Younger Man's part or a tactic in order to throw his game off. While they were both by no means enemies, the seriousness to which these games had become meant that the stakes were high enough to deploy such devious tactics.

After another moment of silent contemplation, the Elder made both his moves.

"Hard to say really," he uttered briefly, taking the first victim off the board.

Pawn takes D5

The Younger Man was choosing the game he wished to play. His eyes barely registered the pawn being taken off the board. To him it was a sacrifice for a greater game being played. What was hard to judge for the Elder, was which game that was.

"Why's that?" he asked back, betraying no emotion that the Elder could tell.

"Variables," The Elder replied, looking over the board as he spoke.

"Such as?"

"The situation outside," The Elder stated with a chuckle.

The Younger Man didn't respond, instead turning his attention back to the board. The Elder watched as his hand reached towards several pieces, before retracting again. He continued this for a few moments, deliberately looking over pawns, bishops, knights, before pulling back and looking over the board again. Eventually, he spoke up and looked at the Elder.

"Fancy going out and checking?" he asked, a mischievous glint in his eye.

"Do you?" The Elder replied, quick and sharp as a knife.

And with that, the situation was defused. Both men erupted into friendly laughter as long, bright smiles erupted over their faces. The tension that was building in the air evaporated in an instance, and with a deep sigh the Elder watched as the Younger Man relaxed once more, making his move.

Knight takes D5

Sure enough, it had been a trap...

It had been rare of late that the subject of their situation had been bought up. The event had been consigned to the mental archives of history, a vague recollection for both men that neither really cared to remember. All that could be said were the base facts: there were warnings from the government that required the building of several bunkers. They were to be stocked with supplies to support a large group for a number of decades, but were largely a protective adventure, prevention being preferred to the cure. However, once the explosions began, there was little time to follow orders. People panicked and threw themselves into half-finished bunkers, thinking only of their own safety and not of any semblance of direction. A panic washed over the populace as men and women turned on each other. There were vicious fights and horrible decisions made, as the government kept trying to maintain a level of control which instead gave rise to a police state. In fact, it had been pure luck that both men had stumbled across one of the completed bunkers, and before they had the chance to help their friends and family, they watched as people burst into flames and melted before their very eyes. They were the only two to enter, and after that no-one else came to join them.

Like most traumatic events, neither man had chosen to discuss it in later times. Indeed, it was simply remembered as a reason to their current predicament. A means that had led to their current end.

Bishop to E2

Pawn to E4

The Younger Man was getting restless again. Obviously, the previous line of questioning had made him hungry for more, and the Elder's attempts to subdue him were temporary at best. He looked back up at the Elder, who was deep in thought over his next move.

"Do you think anyone will come for us?" he asked, the negativity shaking in his voice. "I mean does anyone know we're here?"

Knight takes E4

The Elder just shook his head. "It's hard to say. I'm sure someone will come eventually."

Knight to F4

"Eventually?"

King swaps with Rook, Right

"And if they don't..."

Knight takes E2

The Younger Man was all ears, his eyes focused on the Elder and not on the board, his moves automatic and no longer considered. His breath was heavy, his eyes wide and waiting.

The Elder looked up, his face an ocean of calm and, though slightly less obvious as to not betray his feelings, resignation.

"We just wait..."

Queen takes E2

The Younger Man's move was panicked, throw-away. He had almost stopped caring, getting erratic.

Bishop to G4

The Younger Man looked back immediately into the old, apathetic eyes of the man across from him. For a moment, all they did was sit in silence, waiting for the words to come. Eventually, they did.

"Until it all ends," whispered the Younger Man, the words sour in his mouth.

The Elder just offered a kindly smile and sighed, making his move.

Knight to F6

"Checkmate."

Suddenly, the Younger Man's attention fell back to board. He looked it over, confused, thrown and trying to figure out what was going on. It was true, the Elder had taken him down swiftly and easily. For a moment the Younger Man struggled to comprehend his loss, opening and shutting his mouth as if to produce some sort of retort. It was futile, the game was over, and he had lost.

For his part, the Elder almost looked hurt in victory. He had won, both games one could argue, and for that he felt no great glory but instead empathy for his opponent. He could only watch as the Younger Man kept analysing the board over and over *and over* again, looking for an out, a loophole that would make the game continue. It was no use, he had been sloppy and now was about to pay the price. Finally, he looked up and at the Elder.

"I'm sorry," The Elder mustered silently, and reached under the table. Before he could grab what he had intended though, the Younger Man used his youth to quickly intercept his hand and grab it instead. He pulled it up and put it forcefully onto the table, scattering some of the pieces.

It was a bottle of water. Clear, untainted water, still fresh despite the years. For a moment the Elder could only watch as the Younger Man held onto it, clinging so hard the plastic buckled underneath his fingers. He looked angry, burnt, ready to do something stupid. The tension that had gone was now back and bleaker than ever. Both men sat there silently, before the Younger Man made his move.

He pushed the bottle to the Elder and let go.

The Elder could control himself no longer as he grabbed the bottle and opened it roughly, devouring the water inside like a hungry animal. The Younger Man could only watch with dry lips as some spilled down the Elder's beard, running through the dry wisps that hung off his chin.

After a moment, the Elder sat there and realized his moment of greed. It was his turn to look for words that would not come, but instead the Younger Man just smiled softly.

"Well done."

The Elder just nodded in gratitude, but still felt the guilt lay heavy on his heart.

"How many more do we have left?"

The Elder looked over to where their supplies were kept. There were few bottles, probably less than twenty. Before he could answer he watched as the Younger Man reset the board.

"Well I guess I better win then," he stated, the twinkle returning to his eye, as a grin crept up the side of his face.

The Elder smiled back, and sat back as the chess board was set back up. They had played this game a great many times, and the results were pretty fair. Hopefully one day, he thought to himself, they would no longer need to play though.

"Right. Now I do believe it's my turn."

The Elder smiled and nodded, watching the Younger Man make his first move.

Pawn to B4

Happy As Larry

Larry wasn't happy.

In fact, it would be fair to say Larry was never happy. Nor did he have much reason to be. Life had dealt Larry a harsh hand. School had been a trial, work even more so. His love life was non-existent and his social life wasn't hot to trot either. If Larry bet on red, it would come up black. All this bad luck led to Larry being quite heavily on the side of maudlin.

However, the friends he did have, Brian and Tik, wanted him to be happy. They'd do everything they could to cheer him up, from evenings at the pub to days out to various fun places. However, the pub visits would end for Larry with lost wallets, spilled drinks and mocking rejections from the fairer sex, and as for the days out... well nobody really mentions when Larry was left upside down on a roller-coaster.

But his two best friends were nothing if not determined. They had known Larry all their life and wanted the best for their chum. When Larry was invariably broke, some random bill appearing to strip his assets, they would meet up and discuss ways to increase Larry's fortune. Along with friends Kay and Dick, they would drink heartily and wonder aloud.

"How *do* you cheer someone up with his luck?" Brian asked.

"Ice cream usually works for me," Dick replied.

"You're such a girl," Kay said.

"How about we buy him a hooker?" Tik suggested, drawing strange looks from the others.

Their suggestions continued into the night, ranging from giving him a big hug to more outlandish ideas of hypnosis, usually from the slightly unhinged Tik. However, one evening, around three pints in, one of his ideas took hold.

"Well what about we just, you know, wish upon a star?"

It may have been the beer talking, but the other three found themselves agreeing with Tik's idea. A wish, a simple gesture lost in times of birthday cakes and broken poultry bones, was innocent and easy enough for the four to invoke.

And so, with their livers full of Dutch Courage, they ascended to the highest point in town and looked out onto a cool, clear sky above. It was filled with bright shining stars that gazed back down upon them. It was decided, they would wish good fortune and happiness for their mutual friend/acquaintance Larry.

After a brief argument over what star to wish upon, with Tik dismissing Dick's suggestion as being 'a bit evil-looking', they stood in a circle, held hands and looked up.

"We wish Larry happiness and good luck in the future," They all said, as one, before letting go of each others hands.

And with that, they all retired to their respective beds and waited...

Sure enough, the next day Brian bumped into Larry and there was a noticeable difference in his friend. There was a spring in his step, a joy in his gait, a twinkle in his eye that once was dim.

"You OK Larry?"

"Never better! I had some good news!" Larry exclaimed, before launching into a tale so incredible Brian's jaw nearly dropped clean off.

It seemed that on that morning, Larry woke, well-rested for the first time in his life, to the sound of a knocking at the door. The knocker was a postman, delivering a 'very important letter' for him. The contents turned out to be a substantial cheque from a relative that Larry had never heard of until now. The figures nearly made Brian feel faint, but there was more to come.

"I went into work, feeling a bit better, and my boss saw my chipper mood and gave me a promotion!"

"Why?"

"Apparently I had the look of a 'go-getter'! What's best of all is I can work at home, on flexible hours!"

"Wow... what's the job?"

"Internet researcher!"

"So... you get paid to surf the internet?"

"Yep!"

So as well as being freshly minted and now a professional web-surfer, Larry's fortune also included the phone number of a new girl at work, who shared all his tastes, ideas and quirks, and winning a holiday for 2 at the tropical resort of Banoi, all expenses paid. As Brian listened in astonishment, he couldn't help feel fantastic for his friend Larry, and how everything was coming up in his favour.

But, after relating all his joy and glee, Larry's face turned a shade of worry. When Brian asked, Larry said that he had a call from Tik. Wondering why he didn't, Brian checked his phone to see that it had crashed completely, lacking signal or even a screen anymore.

As for Tik, he had been involved in a terrible and freak accident. While leaving his house, a frozen block of urine had hit him in the back, leaving him both paralysed and smelling of wee. With this, Brian suggested the two visit their friend, but Larry looked grim.

"It probably won't be worth it."

"Why Larry?"

"He's in a coma as well."

Brian didn't understand it, but Larry said they would visit soon. In the meantime, how about celebrating Tik with a trip to the pub, on him?

Brian couldn't help but feel he needed it.

However, once they got there, the pub that Brian, Tik, Kay and Dick had loved for so long was no more. A bizarre fire had broke out, burning the place to the ground and leaving a mere shell behind. This left only one other option, a more expensive and lower-class pub around the corner. Larry though, in his nature, offered to spot Brian for any drinks, especially once Brian's card was eaten by a cash machine.

On arriving at the expensive pub, they found Kay looking forlorn.

"Jesus Kay, you alright?"

Kay was not alright. She recounted how she had not only found out she was pregnant, but she'd also lost all her money through a Nigerian scam and was having to move back in with her parents after her housemates barricaded the flat.

"Why would they do that?" Brian asked.

"Something to do with Cthulhu," Was all Kay could muster in response.

Worse was to come though, as when Brian asked where Dick was, Kay's face turned to ash. Apparently, at the same time as Tik's ice-urine torpedo crippled him, a shit-filled one fell a few miles away, hitting Dick in the face and severing his head clean off.

Brian stood there in utter shock, until Larry arrived gleaming with a tray in hand.

"Who wants cocktails?" He cheered, causing Kay to burst into tears and run away. Larry looked at Brian confused.

"Hormones."

And so, after a few drinks, where Larry found himself propositioned by many women and had people buy him drinks for reasons that were both noble and downright strange, the two friends took stock.

"So, Dick's dead, Kay's life is in ruins and Tik is a comatose paraplegic?"

"Yes Larry."

"Crikey... how about you?"

Apart from a dead phone and a lost bank card, Brian had come out clean so far. But a lack of contact with anyone outside of Larry filled him with a certain ominous dread. So far, this spate of apocalyptic luck had been easy on him, but as Brian thought about what had happened to their companions, he shivered at the prospects awaiting him at home.

As he looked across the table, he saw his friend Larry, the man who life seemed to keep punching in the groin, finally smiling. Not just smiling, beaming with a wonder and euphoria he had never seen from him before. Part of Brian was happy for Larry, but then he thought of what happened to the others.

"I'm just going to use that phone box over there Larry, just to see what's what."

Larry smiled and nodded, before being accosted by several beautiful women wanting to discuss the inner workings of the fantasy film genre with him. While he talked in detail about swords and dragons, he watched as Brian entered the phone box across the street, while a tower crane whirred overhead, slowly carrying a block of granite, several tonnes in weight, with a creaking chain wrapped around it.

Nought to Sixty

The Summer sun was making its descent just as he was coming round. The threadbare blinds of the motel room allowed slender slithers of light to penetrate, bathing him in a few slits of the days last brightness. As he began to come to, he held his hand up to the dusk-shine and stretched out his fingers, looking at the shadow of his hand against the white blinds. He stretched and contracted each finger, dozily intrigued at every bit of movement it gave. Before long, he just crunched it back into a fist and stretched the rest of his body.

The sun was setting, and it was time to go to work.

As the actual day ceased to be outside, his day was just beginning. Dusk was his morning, the first small specks of star-shine his blue sky. When he took the job of a driver one of the requirements was night work.

"Easier to get around," they had told him. "Less people looking for ya."

That was true. Your average Joe didn't care what happened while they slept, as long as they woke up the next day to find a world to still live in. The night was the Devil's playground, where the worst of the worst and the insomniac damned loiter. He saw them all the time, sadly moping around and living their anti-lives. It was a surreal world to be a part of.

He looked around his motel room for his belongings. Thankfully he was a minimalist, and the kind of rooms he stayed in weren't burdened with elaborate furnishings. His clothes were on a side chair, his wallet and keys on the desk next to him. Nothing fancy, just the essentials.

Besides, his most important belongings were in the car outside.

He pulled his jeans on and took stock of his surroundings. The room was part of a service station motel in the North East. One of your generic pump-n-pick-up type deals filled with shops full of nibbles and fast food outlets with high prices. These were the breeding grounds of risky businessmen and weary travellers, going in and out without a hint of life about them.

The motel was the most exciting part of the whole scene. They were rarely populated during the day, with the exception of the odd suit enjoying some afternoon delight with his young secretary. He saw them as they cautiously made their way to the rooms, sometimes catching his eye and immediately looking anywhere else. It was an old joke, but it still made him laugh.

The joy was quickly superseded by the sadness though, as seeing the couples in courtship reminded him of The Girl. He opened his wallet to take a quick glance at her picture that took pride of place within. He drank in her long auburn hair, bright smile and eyes that pierced you all the way to your heart. Since she left for the Welsh coast, he had missed her every day and longed to pick up the phone and call. But it wasn't as easy as that anymore.

Nothing was.

Instead, he threw on his top and got ready to hit the road. The package he had today was to be picked up in a couple of hours, once the normal folk were watching their shows and tucking their kids up in bed. Business hours were over for them, but he was just opening shop.

He took one last look at The Girl and had the urge to get in touch, do something to let her know that was still out there, but thought better of it. It was easier having a memory than trying to chase a future, and he was far too deep to dare bring her down with him.

He put the wallet in his back pocket, picked up his keys and left his room, basked in the final glow of the days light.

The service station had a large area in the centre of it designed to house all the diners from the surrounding food establishments. There, a heady mix of greasy aromas and strong coffee wafted through the air while cleaners dully mopped the floors and shop staff checked their nails and phones.

After killing time with another generic book picked up from the cheap bins, some fantasy joke by a writer named Chris something, he had picked up his usual breakfast: Large burger with a 'Midnight Cola'. He preferred the soft drink over coffee as a liquid pick-me-up, finding coffee too abrasive on the nerves. It made you think too fast and impulsively, which naturally would lead to mistakes. When you were on the road, the last thing you would want to do is something wrong, especially when your cargo was so precious.

Nope, the cola was good enough. Sugary enough to start the motors and sweet enough to taste good. The burger was just meat, protein to give his body the impression that he had eaten something. For such a terrible diet, he was in pretty decent shape mostly in spite of a normal 3 Course Meal. He had enough vitamins and supplements in the compartments of his car to get by, allowing him to get on with the important job of driving.

He finished off his burger and checked his phone. Still no word from the contact. His bosses had told him to give him until past midnight to come or drive away, no point in sticking around. They worked on a tight deadline, and if you didn't adhere to that then there was always another customer on the list. No doubt if they didn't turn up tonight, he'd be given a new destination to head to and dispose the goods there.

No matter. He enjoyed the drives anyway.

As he looked around the stations food court, he took in the late night clientele. A few lonely figures, reading their papers and eating their last meals before setting off. The usual cast of characters were there, truckers on a more legal route than he was, and the ladies of the night competing for their attention and pay packets.

One person did catch his eye though. Far across the room, a strange figure in black was looking in his direction, his hands interlocked in front of him. He couldn't work out whether the figure was looking at him or over him, but still he wondered whether this was the contact he had been waiting for. He made eye contact in order to gain a level of recognition, and gave a subtle nod.

The figure looked away again. He guessed he had been wrong.

The minutes lurched past midnight, and the contact still hadn't shown up. He pulled out his phone and text his employers.

NO SHOW. WHAT NOW?

Seconds passed before he got his answer.

NOTHING YET. TAKE THE NIGHT OFF.

Well this was a rare treat. He hadn't had a night where he hadn't been making a drop in months, usually the demand for the goods being so high that it was a constant journey across the country. He couldn't help smiling to himself about his new found freedom before the reality set in.

Here he was in some nothing service station in the middle of the motorways, alone and in the dark heart of the night. His options were limited as he knew no-one close by, and besides it was far too late to drop in on someone. However, naturally his mind drifted to The Girl. Maybe he could go to her, get in touch and ask if she fancied some breakfast. Offer the pipe of peace and...

No. It was a pipe dream. Besides, by the time he got there dawn would be breaking and she'd barely be awake anyway. It was a folly he didn't want to indulge in.

Ironically, as he thought that, one of the short-skirted ladies shimmied his way. He always tried to not make eye contact with them, instead scrolling mindlessly on his phone in the hopes they'd ignore him. This one didn't seem so easily fooled, and perched herself on his table.

"Hey, looking for some business?"

For a moment he was tempted. She didn't look too bad, not too old nor ravaged by drugs or whatever it was that put her in this position. On the other hand he didn't really want to throw his money away on a cheap fling. He gave a half-hearted smile and shook his head.

"Sure I can't tempt you?"

His eyes drifted away and again caught the glare of the figure across the room. This time he was definitely looking straight at him, his look intense and studious. It freaked him out a little bit, and he barely noticed the prostitute mutter at him and walk away.

He decided to get moving again. The figure was seated near the exit to the car park, so if he wanted something with him there would be his chance. He gave one last look around the complex, seeing as the lady who propositioned him had moved onto a loose-tied suit with more sweat than hair.

Looked like someone was getting some business tonight.

He walked briskly across the table areas and made sure to keep the figure in black in his peripheral vision. If he did want something with him, then now would be the time to find out. He felt himself start to get paranoid about this guys intentions, whether he'd been sent by something. Maybe even his employers. Maybe this whole deal had been some sort of set-up...

As he got close he prepared himself for a conflict. He puffed out his chest and steeled his nerves, clenching his fists in case things got physical.

Instead, as he walked past the figure just sat there and spoke up.

"Drink?"

He stopped and looked back, confused.

"Sorry?"

"A drink. Would you like to join me for a drink?"

The figure gestured to the table where a glass of cola sat untouched. He guessed that the figure had studied his habits and bought him the cola as some sort of introductory measure. At that moment he started to think that maybe this guy was like the lady before, a man looking to proposition him for some sort of sleazy activity. He had seen it go on before, sordid lives converging at anonymous rest stops.

He adopted the same half-smile, head-shake tactic as before.

"Don't worry I want to talk to you, not have sex with you," the figure purred, his eyes glaring up through the top of his sockets.

Now he was intrigued. The idea of this being some sort of ruse played by his employers got even firmer in his mind. He could walk off, get in his car and get away as planned, but something about this figure teased him in.

He took the seat, and had a sip of the cola. Nice and cool, just how he liked it.

"Trucker?" the figure asked, pointing out his arms to the rest of the room.

He shook his head, watching this guy and trying to figure him out.

"Driver then."

"Something like that. You?"

The figure just sat back and took a deep breath. "I'm an observer, an... assistant. A drinking buddy!"

He just nodded again. Something about this Buddy was off.

"I'm guessing business didn't go as planned tonight."

"Nope."

Buddy just nodded as he thought this over. "Guess you got plans then, seeing as you turned down that lovely lady over there."

"Nope."

"Oh."

Buddy paused, then an unnerving smile crept across his face as he pointed towards him.

"You're taken already."

"Nope."

It was true, he wasn't taken in the *literal* sense, although The Girl had taken something of his.

"Oh you're lying. I can tell. It's a gift."

He just shrugged and kept enjoying his drink. The guys act was starting to wear on him already, and he just wanted to finish up and get out.

"So you're a Driver with a Girl... kind of," Buddy concluded. "And you're a Driver with a Girl with nothing to do... what to do, what to do."

"I was thinking of going for a drive," he deadpanned.

Buddy just stonewalled him. "Good plan."

"Thanks."

They just sat there and looked at each other in silence for a moment, the only sound the hum of the cleaners across the hall. As he finished Buddy's cola, he started to prepare to go again.

"Care to make it interesting?" Buddy asked.

He stood up. "What do you mean?"

"Well, you have nothing to do except drive, and you have a Girl somewhere around... let's say the coast."

He shivered. Whoever this Buddy was he had a lot of information for a stranger. He decided to bite the bullet.

"Do you work for East?"

"Nope."

"Carter?"

"Nope."

"Douglas?"

"Nope. Well this is fun! I can see why you did this just now!"

He just looked coldly at Buddy. The man in black was clearly enjoying this but he wasn't anymore. It was like he was playing a game where he didn't know the rules.

"What's your angle then?"

Buddy just looked at him with something that was trying to be a smile. "I just want to make a little bet."

"What kind of bet?"

"Sit down and I'll tell you."

He complied as Buddy continued talking.

"Rest assured I don't work for any of your friends. I'm an independent contractor. Someone who, as I said, likes to assist people like yourself. However such assistance comes at a price."

He nodded. "The cost of a bet."

"Exactly."

"So what are the odds?"

"Straight to business. Good lad."

"What are the odds?" He asked again, firmer than before.

"Well, what you stand to win is this. You'll be freer than you were tonight, given a life of luxury as long as you live and no more dependency on those that employ you."

He listened as Buddy paused for effect, leaning back in his chair.

"And most of all, you'll have The Girl."

He swallowed hard. He didn't know who Buddy was but he knew the buttons to press.

"What's the bet?"

"I bet, that you, cannot get to her before the sun rises."

He thought for a moment to take this in. It was a strange proposition, but a challenging one. Buddy explained for him before he could figure it all out himself.

"From where you are right now you're exactly 5 hours away from where she is. The sun rises in exactly...?"

"5 hours."

"Bingo."

It was his turn to smile now, careful not to show his hand too much or break Buddy's gaze.

"If I lose?"

Buddy waved his hand about as if it didn't matter, giving the full range of theatrics before continuing.

"You carry on as you were, a driver for disreputable people who longs for a Girl he can't have. Oh, except that you definitely can't have her as she'll be dead."

This made him sober up to the whole deal.

"Well, as good as dead. I can't go into the specifics of what me or my... associates, do. But rest assured that should the sun rise and she not be in your range, she won't be. Ever."

He wanted to snap Buddy's head off his shoulders, but it wasn't his style.

"And what if I don't take the bet?" He asked.

"You already have. I'd probably get going if I were you."

He looked at Buddy and felt the rage burn harder than before, but the look in the figures eyes suggested he was deadly serious. There were no other options if The Girl's life was in danger. He needed to get in his car and drive.

He didn't say anything, instead getting up from the table with as much suggestion of violence as he could, never breaking Buddy's gaze. He grabbed his keys and ran for the exit.

The last thing he heard before the doors shut behind him were two, emotionless words:

"Good luck."

The night air was refreshing as he jogged out the service station, sobering him to the situation in hand. It was cooler than normal, the mugginess of the day dissipating away to a brisker dark, almost like desert weather. Perfect driving weather.

His car was ready and waiting for him near the entrance. It wasn't much to look at, but that was by design. Too many police keep an eye out for boy racers at night, so anything that looked sporty and flash would impede his progress exponentially. Instead, his vehicle looked like any generic car-off-the-street, something you'd give your first kid or buy second hand on a budget.

It's appearance was deceptive though, as under the hood it was a beast. Re-tuned and modded to the point of abuse, when it needed power it gave him it's all. Many deadlines had been crushed thanks to a last bout of speed from the bottom of the cars heart.

And speed was what he needed. As he jumped in he checked his watch, seeing it was a little after half past the witching hour. 5 hours. 5 hours to get from here to the where The Girl was. It was certainly doable, just needlessly tight. There was no room for error, one bad traffic light and he'd be behind schedule.

It was time to put his skills to the test.

He fired the engine and swerved his way out the car park. It was dead save for a few overnighters, allowing him to cut through straight to the exit. As he did he checked his fuel gauge: full to the brim. It'd be tight sure, with the likelihood of running on fumes for the last few miles, but like everything else it was achievable. And that was the only thing that he could think of right now, what was achievable.

He said goodbye to the services, and of course Buddy himself, and jumped on the motorway for the first leg of his race. Just him, 300-odd miles and the road.

Just how he liked it.

He switched on the Sat and checked the route. He didn't usually rely on technology for his journeys but it was good to have back up. The Sat told him what he already knew, that this was a simple case of hugging the motorway until he got to the Welsh border. What he didn't like was its estimation: 5 and a half hours. But that was at a leisurely pace that wasn't his style, and half an hour was easy to cut. He put his foot down and threw the gears up, the engine growling along with him.

If he was honest he was scared. Buddy was a weirdo but seemed to be the real deal. There was something menacing about him, about the way he calmly stated his bet and had almost zero emotion to him. Anything he did show seemed to be some sort of well-rehearsed act, it was unnerving. The real question was who did he work for? He had made a lot of enemies in this job and even his bosses were not to be trusted. End of the day though, they had nothing to gain through these cheap threats, his skills were too valuable to them. But Buddy didn't seem to care about any skills or even his position.

He just seemed interested in him and The Girl.

The night did it's best to bring his tension down. The roads were calm and clear, black strips lit by little florescent suns above. At first the unnatural light had made his head hurt, but now it was his own personal sunshine, never clouded by weather and always there to shine down on him. It was the little things like that which kept him sane.

The peace that came with it usually allowed him time to think, time to put his tasks in order and keep on top of things. The only problem with that was it also gave him time to think about The Girl, and tonight that subject was stronger than ever. He began to curse himself for ever pushing himself away from her. They had their disagreements but the way he vanished from her life was stupid. He didn't want to, quite the opposite, but given the emotional weight behind the situation he had no choice. Instead he drove, and now look where he was.

No, tonight wouldn't be a contemplation night. He needed to concentrate on the drive, the time. He needed something to distract him from the knot that was forming in his stomach. From thinking about The Girl.

Tonight would be a radio night.

He flicked it on and was greeted by the smooth sounds of some rock band. It was a strange sound, quite different from what he'd ever heard before, but it was doing the job of taking his mind away from dark places. Instead as the song played on, his eyes stayed fixed on the road and his foot pushed harder on the accelerator.

He could do this. He was *sure* he could do this.

"That was Vendetta, with their latest hit single. One that's definitely for you night owls out there. Anyway, it's 2 o'clock which means you're with me, Easy E, for the next 4 hours until the sun shines in the sky. Strap yourself in, it's gonna be a Hell of a ride."

The DJ didn't know how right he was.

The good news was he was making incredible time. He had been punching the engine hard and it had been responding in kind, keeping the speed high on the dial and never looking back. The roads had kept their end of the bargain as well, keeping nice and clear of any potential obstacles. The only issues he ever had were lorries deciding to dominate the lanes, or the occasional drunk driver who would put more risk than needed into the drive.

But tonight was a good night, and he was feeling pretty good about himself. He could most likely get to The Girl before the sun even came close to popping it's dazzling head over the horizon. He had shaved miles off his journey through sheer force, and was already seeing the finish in sight.

The only thing that did bother him was the equal fast rate in which the fuel was easing it's way down. He had known it would be a squeeze, but seeing it in the cold reality made his heart beat a little faster.

It was all fine though. He was still confident and almost cocky in his estimations. He could even stop off somewhere and pick up a lunchtime treat if he wanted. But he'd fallen down that rabbit hole before. Pride always came before a fall, especially in the driving business. He remembered a colleague who was so sure he was going to hit a deadline he decided to take a more visually pleasing route.

Suffice to say, he didn't drive anymore.

So no, in spite of the confidence that was building inside of him he wouldn't push his luck. Time was still a factor, even though the Sat was now agreeing with his predicted arrival, and the fuel was a constant worry.

But the tunes were keeping him in a focussed mood, and everything was going according to plan.

"And we've got our first caller of the night," Easy E announced on the radio, "What ya gotta say Buddy?"

"Well, I just want to wish luck to a friend who's out on a drive tonight," a familiar voice intoned. "And I want him to know that I'm ready and waiting for him to arrive on time."

He shivered as the words sank in. Buddy was taunting him and it made him more alert. That something that he had felt before came back, and paranoid thoughts began to estimate how Buddy might try and sabotage his ride. As a broody, doom-tinged song played as his "dedication", he put his foot down and pushed the car even harder.

It was stupid hubris on his part.

From under the bonnet smoke began to spew out. He immediately knew the radiator was overheating from the pressure and he had gone too far in his efforts to cut his time down. He wanted to push on, but knew any further force on his part would cause an end-game.

No, he had to pull over, and cool the car down.

He skidded into the lay-by and grabbed a bottle of water from the back seat. A quick turn of the key killed the engine and he heard it cough out of life, leaving behind a mist that seemed to drift away casually as if to taunt him further.

Jumping out, the smell made him almost gag. It was as if the car was a corpse deep in the stages of its own decomposition, giving off foul odours to cry that it had given up. But he knew it wasn't dead yet, just in pain. He lifted the bonnet, ignoring the heat that seared his fingertips, and poured the water liberally over the insides. More smoke spat back at him, but after a few minutes it had trickled down to a more conservative volume. But these were minutes he couldn't afford to lose, and cursed with impatience as he checked that everything was in tune and ready to go again.

After half an hour, he was finally satisfied. Well, as much as he could have been.

He had lost time. Not just any time, a chunk of time that now seemed like an abused gift. He had started to put all his chips on one number, forgetting the odds were always changing and not in his favour. Part of his mind wondered if Buddy had anything to do with this turn of events. There was nothing suspicious when he looked at the engine, nothing had been tampered with, but something just irked at him.

Now was the time not just to make speed, but to break it. He still had miles and miles of road ahead of him and being frugal in terms of fuel and legality were no longer options.

Once back behind the wheel, he threw the car back into life and kept his foot down until it screamed along the motorway again. There was no choice in the matter; if he was to reach The Girl he was looking at a triple digit drive, damn the consequences.

The world seemed to blur around him as he drove. Everything washed away in a blitz of colour and shape that was lost to the velocity of the vehicle pushing him. All he saw in his sights now was the road, his mind thinking several steps ahead like a chess player. He had a lot of time to carve away and too much road to take it.

And all he could think about was The Girl.

She was now firmly in his minds eye, as if she were travelling with him. She always had of course, not just in his mind but in his heart. Every journey she was by his side, reminding him that in the end she was still there, and somewhere she was still thinking of him. Sometimes, he liked to hope that she was still waiting for him, to return and finally tell her everything he thought and felt.

It took a few moments before he noticed the lights in his rear view mirror. He knew exactly what they were when he saw them; blue and angry and out to slow him down. He had had dealings with the Police many times, those moments where he and the car were punching a little too close to their weight, but he always managed to sneak away with a telling off.

However, now there would be no telling off. He was blazing along and the Police car behind him wasn't pleased. But it was about to get angrier, as there was no way he was slowing down.

Its sirens wailed behind him, screaming at him to stop and face justice. Right now The Girl and Buddy's bet was shouting louder though, and he started to think about how the Hell he could get rid of this distraction.

The Sat suggested a number of options; side roads and country diversions which would allow him some creativity. The Police car was maintaining speed with him, but he knew that if he pushed a little harder, at the risk of the already boiling engine and evaporating fuel tank, he could lose them.

The motorway gifted him a turn-off and he saw this as his opportunity. He steadied his hands on the wheel, very aware of the small window he had in which to make his move. As he approached, he straddled the chevrons between the turn-off and the rest of the motorway. The Police car behind him weaved, trying to guess his choice. It was 50-50, and his window was getting smaller.

He swerved back toward the motorway, dangerously close to clipping the dividing barrier. The lights behind him kept flashing, the siren still screaming.

The Police had made the right call. They were still behind him.

There were options ahead to try the trick again, but the risk was too high at this speed. He needed a better plan and he needed it now. The Police car behind him was now desperately trying to keep up, and from all his experiences before he knew it wouldn't be long before the Police car would have company.

Another turn was on the way, leading to some country roads that hadn't seen light since the dusk before. If there was going to be any chance of him losing the Police, this would have to be it.

He went for the same bluff but was more cautious this time round. The Police were still behind him as he ducked and dived around the narrowing roads, flanked by high trees and dark land. The only lights were carefully dotted at mean lengths, enough to pass a safety test but still giving you moments of tension.

But the pitch black gave him an idea. It would cost, but it would give him some breathing space.

Using one last burst of speed, he punched the car forward and hit the lights. The Police behind lost all sight of him as he went past the last streetlight for a mile or so. Pushing forward in the dark, he grabbed the handbrake and turned fiercely, the car skidding forward sideways at this point. He watched as the Police car fast approached and turned his lights back on so they were facing them. They swerved as he put his foot down again and headed off in the opposite direction. A few miles later, and he was in the clear.

But he was going the wrong way, and the clock was ticking.

A few quick turns and some strategic side roads had found him back on the motorway and only 2 hours away from his deadline. Everything was playing against him though; the fuel was burning faster than he could drive, and when he did push it to the limit his engine roared back at him to remind him of the earlier meltdown. Both had demanded he cut his enthusiasm down, and he had eventually reluctantly complied. Luckily the fierce speed at which he had driven before had made up what he had lost, but only just. He was looking at hitting the wire hard.

This meant looking over some new options. He knew as soon as he'd hit the Welsh border he'd have to deal with the toll, and that wasn't going to happen if he had to get to The Girl on time. Instead, more side roads and dark routes were in his future, and this meant even more conservative driving. His nerves were starting to shred, and he knew he had to do something that he had been putting off.

The Girl's number was still waiting on his phone, untouched. He had acquired it in better times and had kept it out of sentiment. It had teased him constantly, wondering why he hadn't just been a man and called. It was a weight around his neck, and he was finally ready to cast it off due to the circumstances he was in. If he called her and let her know she was in danger, then he could rest a little easier. It would be awkward, they hadn't spoke in a while, but it was no longer about anything emotional or otherwise.

He tapped the number, and waited for an answer.

Voice mail.

Of course. It was the dead hours of the morning and her phone was most likely turned off. Sure he could leave a message but say what? "Look out there's some weirdo who may or may not hurt you"? Buddy's bet was vague, but his intent was ominous.

He cancelled the call, and got back to the drive in hand.

The moment came when he had to cross over into Wales, and navigate the system of B roads and country lanes. His main problem would be weaving through those that were sharing the network with him. Smaller roads meant more build-up, but it was still early enough that he could skirt safely around it. He needed to maintain his speed, and it wasn't clement within these parts. Not only that, but as soon as he entered the smaller roads traffic lights and speed cameras began to rear their ugly heads. It seemed like every few miles he went, he was greeted by a flash that would light up the area. After a while he was the subject of so many photo's he could have made a modelling career out of it.

Most of the lights went in his favour, but soon one stretch of road gave him a warning. Ahead the lights went from Amber to Red, and a car on the opposing road was ready to take advantage. He started to gauge whether there would be a contact point, keeping his hands steady on the wheel and his foot ready to act. The car was going slightly slower than he was, but making good distance. If he kept going, he would just pass in front of it.

He had done it a thousand times and got it just right, but now the moves went a little quicker than planned. As both cars hit the crossroads, he was too close for comfort near the other. A quick spin of the wheel, and veered *just* out the way. All he could do as he straightened up was watch in his rear view mirror as the other car braked hard, skidded across the road and mounted the curb, the driver blaring his horn in anger.

He couldn't help but think how lucky the driver was to be able to hit his horn.

Every light was treated with the same degree of hostility, but luck was on his side as no more drivers were appearing. Yet. The time was ticking closer to a more sociable hour and he was edging closer to his deadline. His fuel was burning and his engine was close to setting itself on fire as well.

And all he could think about was The Girl.

When his phone rang, he nearly crashed into a nearby wall. Upon answering he almost wished he had.

"How's your journey?" Buddy asked.

"Go fuck yourself."

Buddy ignored him, instead reminding him of the time left. "I hear there may be an earlier rise this morning, clear sky and all that. Red Sky in the morning..."

"I've still got time."

"You have. You have until the sun pokes his head up in..." Buddy paused, either for effect or to genuinely work out the time. "1 hour. Time to knuckle down I think."

He just ignored him. He had to keep on driving, keep focused on the road ahead.

"Well don't worry. I'm sure that when you reach her you'll see her straight away. Right in front of your eyes."

He only noticed that Buddy had put the phone down after a few minutes silence. Everything was now far too close for comfort; his fuel gauge had flushed everything it had away and was now ticking near empty, and the roads were getting tighter and more populated.

There was more adventure in his movements now, more risk being thrown in front of him. The constant reminder of a glowing sky in front of him was making him nervous. What if he had misjudged his time? What if the Sat, now going against him again, was right? What would 'Buddy' do to The Girl.

He had to push on. He had to make it. Not for him, for her.

She was all that mattered now.

Dawn was quickly making its presence known, but he was close. Minutes were ticking away faster than he could drive, and all he had in the tank were fumes. But it would be enough, it had to be.

He had never felt tired before but now his eyes were heavy and his body was weak. Suddenly his diet and night-time profession had caught up with him, assaulting him and reminding him of the stupidity of it all. He had only taken it to get away, remove himself from the lives of those around him and vanish into the ether. And the only reason he had done that was to keep himself away from The Girl. It was the best thing to do, for both of them. No more bad vibes and unsaid words. Instead the open road would be his companion and she could forget about him.

It was a dumb move that he had regretted every day.

But now fate was determined to force his hand. Buddy's bet had made him go back to her, go back and re-connect in one way or another. The gun had been put to his head and the only choice he had was to comply. He would go to her, he would tell her how he felt and most of all, he would save her. He would be the hero.

They would still be in each others lives.

The seconds were dwindling as he searched for her road. The path was littered with high streets full of people prepping for the day ahead and the world waking up. Every moment he was swerving and braking in order to stop himself from destroying some shop window. The sun was threatening in the sky, ready to get up and announce itself to the world.

Everything was so close, too close. His car was hurting now, pushed so far that after it was relieved of it's duty all it would be good for would be retirement. But right now he needed it to go that little bit further. This was the last job it would ever need to do for him, and it was the most important.

He reached her road and powered down, with her house right near the end. He kept watch of too many things at once; the road, the Sat, the clock and the sky. All were jostling for his attention, all were reminding him of what he needed to do. Road. Sat. Clock. Sky. Road. Sat. Clock. Sky. AS he hit the accelerator a bit harder his phone rang. Buddy's number.

No.

He still had time. He still had a few seconds. He was nearly there. Road. Sat. Clock. Sky. The phone kept ringing it's tune in his ear. Road. Sat. Clock. Sky. It kept singing to him, demanding he answer. Road. Sat. Clock. Sky. Phone.

Back to the road, stretching ahead.

Back to the Sat, telling him he was out of time.

Back to the clock, telling him he still had a few seconds.

Back to the sky, which was glowing ominously.

Back to the phone, which kept ringing.

Back to the road. Where The Girl stood.

Right in the middle of the road.

Right in his path.

He braked. He turned. He saw her beautiful vision hurtle toward him as he spun the wheel again and felt himself thrown in his seat.

The car flipped and rolled violently down the road. His body churned inside the metal husk that was being beaten this way and that. The phone was crushed into silence, the engine giving one last cry for help before coughing itself dead. It crashed harder against the tarmac before settling on it's roof with his body inside, unconscious.

The last thing he saw was The Girl, running toward him. The beautiful vision.

The sky was getting dimmer outside, the last pieces of light glittering through the curtain. There was nothing left for the day to tell, it was time to give in to the night once again.

The dusk was here to take over and was easing itself into action. Easing itself into a world of seedy business types, ladies promoting their personal wares and, of course, drivers. Whether they be truckers escorting a load from one end of the country to another, or the enigmatic types who drove for more unsavoury types.

They all awoke at this time, much like he did.

He held his hand up to the curtain and stretched it out. It was painful, each bone cracking under the pressure of movement, but as he looked at the silhouette, it was held by her hand. Her soft fingers gently putting his hand back down, back to where it wouldn't hurt.

The two of them looked content in the room, he thought, finally at some sort of peace. Would their story have a happy ending? Who knew. The Driver had broken many bones and suffered much damage in the crash, and all The Girl could do was look after him, whatever that meant.

But for him, the bet was over and The Driver had won. Good for him. Sometimes the underdog had to come through. Not everyone could fall, some had to rise. Even if that came at a great cost.

For a Driver though, walking was over-rated anyway. He had lived with wheels for most of his life.

So yes, that story was over and it was time to find another person to assist. Whether it be in the form of a bet or another, more enticing offer.

As the figure in black sauntered down the hospital corridors, he thought about how many people had wishes or dreams in each room.

He'd bet there were quite a few.

In The Room With Rosie

For you to get a better perspective on matters, let me tell you how my father died.

When I was nine years old, my old man passed away. For the time that passed afterwards, my mother, bereft of the floods of tears one gets in emotional situation due to the utter shock, told me that he had died in a car accident.

"Daddy got in a bit of trouble and hurt himself very badly," Was how she eloquently put it.

She killed herself three months later, ironically in a car, smothered in carbon monoxide.

It wasn't until I was sixteen that my older brother Larry, or Lisa as he… she likes to be known now, told me the truth. Apparently my old man had a life outside the suburban riches that he had acquired through his business. He regularly went to various massage parlours and fetish clubs and strung himself up while a PVC clad blonde whipped him. I believe they call it auto-erotic asphyxiation… Anyway one session went a little too far and it wasn't until the dominatrix noticed that Daddy's rampant masturbating had suddenly stopped that she realised he had clocked himself outta the game.

No wonder my brother became my sister if our Dad was that fucked up. I mean how would you feel if you were told your old man was found dead, naked, with only a gimp mask and a leather strap around his neck?

Me though? Well I was already a rational, rampant, rebellious little rascal myself when I found out. My mind was already moulded by maternal suicide, a sizable inheritance and dip-shit relatives who became my legal guardians. The shame of your brother being a degenerative freak meant that I was smothered in a world of brightness and candy floss. Getting so called 'protection' from the real world. Of course, that type of parenting leads only so far before the clichéd effect takes place.

Anyway, I digress. Point is my Dad was a sick pervert who died jacking off to a fat whore with rolls of fat spilling out from beneath black PVC. No wonder I have no empathy for poor Rosie here.

Right now, in this sparse environment known only as a cheap motel room off the motorway, dear Rosie sits buck naked with one of those speciality gimp masks clamped onto her head. It's one of those ones that, funnily enough, my old man wore in his last hurrah, designed to restrict the amount of oxygen you receive. Funny how things work out eh?

Unfortunately the air in there is running out and Rosie is getting woozy. Brent has been gone for an hour and he has the key, so all I can do is wait and watch as she slowly chokes in front of me. It would be a distressing scenario for any person involved, like those tense scenes you see in a film, where the hero is up against the clock to save the damsel in distress. In this case though, I don't give a shit and Rosie isn't a damsel in distress. She's a hooker.

Like I said, funny how things work out…

Fact of the matter is this. I work as a fixer. While most people fix plumbing or electrics or even bricks and mortar, I fix people's lives. You got a problem? Call me and my associates. We're not assassins nor are we mob hit-men. We are simply people who you hear about from a friend of a friend, people who clear up any inconveniences that are disrupting your lifestyle. As you can probably imagine, most of our clients are names that could get into trouble if the lurid details of their life came out.

We, by whom I mean me and my associates, have seen it all. The love child of a randy MP, the dyke who will scream about her Sapphic affair with a high profile actress and the Royal with a few too many skeletons in his gay little closet. Usually the job doesn't involve any real violence, it just isn't my way, but sometimes you gotta get a little rough.

In the case of Rosie here, that means a little retroactive justice.

Don't ask me why the idea came up, because you probably already have your own answer. Fuck, if Freud were here now he'd be having a field day. I'm not one to come out and deny my subliminal thoughts on vengeance and whatnot; I just do what I do.

Anyway the back story on this little Godot-style scenario is as plain and simple as it usually is. A movie star, lets call him Dave, had been enjoying regular sessions with Rosie here, but then decided to become loving father to his wife and kids. Rosie of course takes umbrage to this removal of steady income, and goes the route most fucks to the stars take and blackmails the shit out of Dave. Dave hears about us, hires us and asks us to remove Rosie.

Hence, me in a cheap motel room, with Rosie slowly losing consciousness in a leather gimp mask, while Brent goes AWOL with the key.

Actually I suppose you're wondering how we got from there to here. Well, to be honest, it's long, boring and not worth taking the time to tell. Suffice to say I'm bored out of my mind and seeing a dying prostitute makes you get a little introspective. Especially given my past.

I told you knowing how my Dad died would give you a greater insight into things.

Maybe this is Gods way of telling me something, making me face the demons that are inhabiting my mind. Forcing me to accept my heritage and confronting it rather than ignore it. But the apathy that I feel with this and my past voids the whole point of the exercise. If I am supposed to learn something from Rosie here that I don't already know, then why is she still dying? Surely God, this big powerful being, would say 'well he's learnt his lesson and so everyone can go home ok now'? I mean, it's not even like I could help her if I wanted. That mask is on to stay.

I dunno. Right now Rosie is a symbol of everything I hate. The seedy underbelly that lurks within society, the perversions of so-called 'normal' people which are hidden from public view. Maybe there is symbolism to be seen, as she lies in the foetal position, the life slowly draining out of her while I sit here and watch, not for pleasure but out of pure boredom. Let me get this straight. I am not enjoying it by any means, but it's been a while and I've already looked over the garish colourings of the room and taken in the view from the window. All that is left to look at is Rosie and her slow painful death. If I took joy in that I would be fucked up.

Like I said, she's a symbol, and her slow perishing could represent my own slow, moral death in this world of fetishism and dark sexual practice. I never got into that whole world to be fair; I'm a straight and narrow missionary type of guy. The closest I get to freaky sex is Doggie Style. Can't say the same for my brother, slash, sister. After Dad's little misadventure Larry became obsessed with the whole underworld and then got lost in it himself. Suddenly he found his feminine side through a series of hardcore ass hammerings and became Lisa, a freaky faux-Barbie that opens her ass to any paying trucker.

I don't hate him… her for it though. She's my brother after all. I'm just saying we siblings became two different sides to one fucked up coin. LarryLisa the sexual deviant, me the emotionless void.

Relationships just never happened for me. I could just never commit to one. All that love and romance stuff was doused in jealousy and, if I admit it to myself, a fear of becoming like my Father. Bored of the same old, same old sexual routine and trying some other piece of cake. Like when you eat all the sushi you can get but crave some Fugu.

So I dated here and there without maintaining a long term partnership. I'm happy to say I'm a good looking guy with a charming personality, so I could if I wanted to. But it just doesn't interest me. I don't sleep around though, it's more the company that matters to me. Someone to wake up next to, in order to combat the feelings of being alone. That's the one emotion that does get to me, loneliness. It's a pain but sometimes you just crave social interaction otherwise you'd get cabin fever.

Maybe that's what Rosie represents? The ability to spend time in the company of another but, due to restrictions, not being able to have that social interaction. Ironic really…

She's begun to squirm, which is slightly disconcerting. We chained her up which took some persuading, so she can't just get up and run naked out the door to be saved by some passing motorist. It's probably desperation as the air becomes thicker within her death mask. I mean her wrists are starting to bleed with her pulling them against the steel of the cuffs. It's tough to watch now but hard to ignore, the bloody elephant in the room. The muffled screams which turned to tears have become gibbering now, inaudible but definitely tinged with fear.

Again, Brent has the key. It's been nearly two hours now and he's not been back. My mobile is silent and my expectations are fading. I'm steadily getting the feeling that I've been left here to baby-sit a dying whore while my associate collects the cash from Dave. I'd be angry if I didn't expect it.

Problem with Brent is that he's unreliable. Scratch that, he's a coke addict, so of course he's unreliable. Only reason I agreed to work with him on this particular job was that he was the first one to pick up. Nothing else beyond that, just sheer blind luck.

I'd worked with him before with a guy named Willy. Can you imagine the amount of mileage we got joking with that name? Anyway, it was a simple case of removing some immigrants from the country, but Brent got itchy and abandoned me and Willy with a van load of Arabs near the border. I got out; Willy stayed in and suffered for it. Brent literally took the money and ran.

So why bother calling him again? Don't know, maybe because of my apathy towards everything, it didn't really bother me that he nearly got me killed. I mean, it's not that I don't trust him. I don't trust anyone.

To some people, Hell is many things. Hell can be sin. It can be eternal torment both physically and mentally. It can be a lake of fire where tiny little imps poke and prod you with pitchforks while you cry. It can be loss, isolation, death, depravity and debauchery. It can be everything you fear or an overload of what you love. To me, to quote Sartre, Hell is other people.

When you grow up in an environment where you're smothered by them, constantly affirmed and never given any time of your own, you either become spoilt or resent it. Shrinks say people who crave social interaction are low on self esteem, not confident enough to be on their own. Guess that makes me the most confident man on the planet.

I live alone, drink alone and eat alone. Bar the fleeting romances, work colleagues or stars of the world that I have to rub shoulders with to do my job, I live a solitary existence and enjoy it. Maybe that exacerbates my hatred, or phobia, of others. Maybe it breeds my lack of feeling towards people like Rosie. Who knows, I'm not a shrink.

Some of you may hate me right now. I mean if I look from the outside, this all looks rather callous. Rosie lays there, barely moving, barely even twitching, and I do nothing. I'm not even watching anymore, just waiting for something to happen. Making mental somersaults in my mind to entertain myself.

To you though, I must seem a monster. A person, whore or not, needs my help and I just sit here doing nothing. Nothing but watch, what a sick and depraved individual I am! How can I not alleviate the pain of another human being? How can I let her lie in an undignified state, losing all signs of life in such a depraved way, while I just muse on my life? Am I a selfish man? A cold man?

Let me spin it another way for you...

Rosie, while a lovely, beautiful, young girl, is a whore. A prostitute, a street walker, a woman who sells her body to make a quick buck. Now, be honest when I ask you this, for I will know if you are lying... do you care about her? I mean really? If you saw her on the street, living that life where respect and dignity are traded for a quick fuck in a back alley to score some cash. A life where a cycle of fucking and spending repeats itself ad nauseam because once she got in she realised she couldn't get out. I mean if she wanted another job what does she say as previous experience? Personal Gratification Supplier?

Take away the fact that right now, she is a victim. That she is dying and in a very bad, very sick scenario. She is a hooker. In a woman's eyes she is a common slut and in a man's eyes... something to fuck, something to use. She's a commodity, a piece of flesh that gets what she deserves. How many stories do you hear of whores getting murdered, slaughtered, raped, pillaged and damaged beyond recognition? How much empathy do you have for them?

Judge not lest ye be judged.

She's definitely stopped moving now. Most likely unconscious, the last shreds of life flittering away as the air in her death mask turns toxic.

As you can probably imagine, death doesn't scare me that much, which I suppose is scary within itself. I mean if you don't fear death, what can you fear? Death represents the ultimate end, the unavoidable destination; it is something that all of us should fear realistically.

But of course, in the world of human nature, I am far from realistic. A bitter caricature created by an uncaring society. Boo-hoo poor me and all that bullshit.

Truth is, I've seen death and seen that when it really comes down to it, it's nothing. You essentially fear something that you will never know, never mentally experience. Death just happens and you, no pun intended, live with it. You can't stop it, you can't change it, it's the end.

The fear, I guess, comes from not knowing. Is there a God? An afterlife? Will I see my Mum and Dad reunited in Heaven, her in an apron and him in a gimp suit, living out their respective fantasies? Will I be born again into another body, my soul transported to another plane, in order to live a life again, or even this life again, on and on until the end of time?

Or do we just simply die. That's it, game over. One minute you're thinking of what you're doing tomorrow and the next, well... nothing. No more. You just lay still and rot, feeding the worms with your celestial shell.

Maybe that's why I don't fear death. Not because I don't fear anything, but because in the end it's an escape. It's something to embrace from the monotony that is real life.

In essence, I'm doing Rosie a favour.

So what now? How does this end? Rosie is well on her way out now, hope but a flicker of light in the ether. Her body pale and still under the sick light of the bulb above.

Do I suddenly have a change of heart, become the hero and pull her back from the brink of death? Or do I pick up the key to the room, the only one I have, and walk away leaving a fake alias and a dead body for the cleaner to find. Will there be a happy ending to this macabre tale?

...

What do you think?
What do you want?

The Bird Cage

From what he could recall, it had been a good day until then.

Nothing out of the ordinary like, say, a lottery win or finding yourself in bed with a couple of open-minded super models, but the sort of good day where everything seemed to be going right. Waking up refreshed, getting to work on time and breezing through the tasks you were given and, of course, beating the crowds at the deli and getting the perfect sandwich. Yes, the day had treated Gary well so far, so naturally it would all have to turn to shit.

He had been walking back to the office, sandwich freshly eaten and motivation for the day up and ready, when he had taken the usual shortcut. The deli he had made his favourite was a few streets away, and if he was honest the walk took up most of his hour, but the results were worth it and by utilising the odd side street you could carve off the time. This was one of those side streets, grotty sure, but short enough to stride through and get to the other side, where civilisation waited. He had seen many a homeless person there, begging for change and looking generally beaten down by the world, but like many other people in the fast nature of the city, Gary listened to his headphones and ignored them. If he would think about it, that would be the last bad decision he would make. The deli, the shortcut and ignoring those below eye-line, all things that would come to haunt him.

Like many of the unseen masses, this one was dressed in dirty, unwashed rags and had the look of a crackhead that hadn't slept for weeks. Maybe they were, maybe they weren't, as Gary walked briskly past the last thing he remembered before blacking out was seeing the throngs of people stride by the exit to the alley, as ignorant to him as he was to the tramps below.

It was the cold that first woke him up. The chill that stung his cheeks and caused his skin to recoil with goosebumps. Luckily he was still dressed in his overcoat, bought for him at Christmas as a warning by his Mother against the 'cold winds that were coming'. Strangely, Gary felt himself pull against it in order to protect himself from the wind, as his eyes lurched open. His head felt several sizes too big, and the sharp pain that suddenly came from the back of his head helped him regain some sort of consciousness. Gary opened his eyes slowly, as if waking from a particularly vivid dream, and looked forward.

In front of him were bars, yellow in colour and latched horizontally and vertically together with enough space in between to fit your hand. But it wasn't that which Gary first noticed, it was the sky beyond it. It was a rich blue, sporadically filled with clouds that drifted idly by, and most importantly for Gary, it was at an angle.

At that moment more of his senses started to come to. He found himself crouched down, limply leaning back against something. As the wind continued to blow against him and the clouds swam past, Gary began to turn to see what he was leaning against.

As he did, he was presented with the sight of more of the yellow latched bars, and beyond that a 250 feet drop to the ground below. In an instance, all of Gary's senses exploded and he found himself lunging away from the bars, screaming in terror and causing the cage he was in to swing wildly around. He suddenly felt his legs warm up as the piss began to soak them, and for a moment he thought he was going to be sick as he steadied himself against the bars surrounding him. The cage he was in wasn't big enough to stand in, and was barely wide enough to turn in, but all Gary was concentrating on was the chilling drop, separated only by the thin sheet of metal below his feet. The cage stopped swinging and centred itself, and Gary felt himself hyperventilating and shaking like a very vulnerable leaf.

It was then that he heard the tinkling of a ringtone from his pocket. For a moment he thought he had gone mad, but on and on it sang its generic song, and eventually Gary steadied his nerves for a moment to pick it up. It wasn't his phone, and the number had no name to identify itself. Gary pressed a button and answered.

"How's the view?"

Gary couldn't answer; he was still in a deep sense of shock, so the voice spoke again.

"Take a look down, if you can. Behind you, to the right."

Gary turned and could see the top of a high story office block just below him. It was probably about forty feet from where he was, but he could make out the three figures who stood there. Two were dressed in what appeared to be suits, while the person they were flanking was shorter and in a thick wooly coat. He gave a wave, and Gary noticed he was watching him with a pair of binoculars.

"Know who I am?"

Gary shook his head.

"Answer me Lad, my eyes aren't that good."

"N... no."

"Well you bloody should," the voice responded calmly. It was old and had a harsh East London tint that Gary thought died out in the 70s. "Because you know my bloody wife."

For a moment Gary had a bit of clarity, but before he could answer the voice spoke up again.

"I'm going to leave you up there for a bit, think about what you've done. Give you a chance to get your bearings. Plus let's me get some lunch. Afterwards we'll speak more about my wife, and more importantly my money."

And with that the phone went dead, and the voice below gave another friendly little wave, before walking off with his suits in tow. Gary could only watch as they entered a door, and vanished off the rooftop. After a moment of hysterics he finally was sick, watching his perfect sandwich splatter against the bars of the cage and slowly rain down far, far below where he stood crouched, the cage he was in swinging slightly in the wind.

In his head, it seemed like only yesterday.

He was in a bar after work, one of the jolly's the lads enjoyed doing to unwind after a weeks hard graft. There was a fund that was dipped into at the start of each week, a tenner here and there, but usually that went in the first round and the rest was taken from residual cash they had been saving up for something important.

The bar itself was a garish affair, all neon signs in the otherwise dark atmosphere. One of these places where the lighting was all mood and that mood, apparently, was straight out of the 80s. Class wasn't the order of the day and judging by most of the clientèle, fellow business types and ladies in high heels and short dresses, it wasn't required.

Gary already had several cocktails and a litre of shots in his system when he saw her. She was almost stereotypical in her good looks, blonde and with a figure that curved in all the right places. He didn't want to say some of it was surgical, but it was hard to argue against the case. In any case it didn't matter, as he had caught her giving him 'the look'.

But he wasn't the sort of guy to act on 'the look'. Often he had been at these bars with the guys and found himself getting it from all manner of ladies, and the guys had nudged and winked at him to pursue it. But for Gary it felt a bit too... seedy. A bit too much of a game that he didn't enjoy playing. Besides he was a shy young fellow, with only a few girls in his own history and one which didn't involve the usual meat market scenes.

Therefore, he decided to play his usual tactic: prop up the bar and wait for them to come to him. At least if she did, she was more interested than intrigued.

Finally after a while, most of which spent waiting to get the barman's attention, Gary looked in the mirror and saw the plump lips and shining hair make their way to his right. As he looked round to greet her the barman finally arrived.

"Good timing," she said breathlessly. It made Gary laugh, and from there on he ordered them both a drink and began to smile back at her.

Gary woke up again with a start.

He had passed out, most likely due to the fear. Instead of leaning against the cage though he was slumped in the middle of it, staring down at the round steel floor that separated him from a sheer drop. Gary felt his heart start to speed up again, but took a deep breath and tried to compose himself. It helped that the air up there was brisk and clean, helping de-fog his mind from the screams and shouts of panic that filled it. He clenched his eyes shut and opened them back up looking at the sky above him.

What he saw didn't allay his fears too much. There was a thick steel crane hook that held the cage up with a thicker steel chain. The cage dangled about 3, maybe 4 feet from the hook, and along the cranes arm there were a few more feet of chain left to drop him even further. The crane itself was one of those tower ones you saw at building sites, the ones that created the giant monoliths where big business was done. Gary tried looking to see if there was anyone at the controls, but as far as he could see the booth was empty. It was just him and the sky.

His first instinct was to call out for help, but the crane was positioned deep in industrial territory, and even if he did try and call out he doubted his voice would reach anyone down below. He felt himself starting to panic again and started taking longer, deeper breaths to slow down his heart rate. It was hard though, every time he opened his eyes they were drawn to the frightening distance between him and the dirt below.

He could barely move for fear of rocking the cage. Slowly turning, Gary noticed a door built into the cage wall where he assumed he had been placed inside. It looked solid enough, but it didn't stop Gary's paranoia going into overdrive at the thought that maybe he had been leaning against that. Maybe, it had snapped open; and maybe, he would have woken up plummeting down, becoming nothing more than a man-shaped Pollack on the surface below.

Gary reached into his pocket again and produced the phone. He checked the time, but it was showing 2 in the morning, definitely wrong. He wanted to throw it out, to spite the person who had been mocking him before, but sense came to him first thankfully.

For a moment he just stayed crouched there, soaked in urine-stained trousers, the smell of vomit coming from the wall of the cage to his left. Luckily, the wind was in his favour, blowing any sensory violations away from him. He needed to think, maintain a sense of calm, get a sense of his options.

Gary crouched still there in the cage for a long time, the wind picking up and the cage swaying slightly more with each gust.

They woke up next to each other much as they had every time they had met. Their eyes opening slowly to reveal themselves, and then their bodies meeting in the middle in a deep embrace. They would stay there, in each others arms, in a moment that seemed to last forever.

Ever since they had met in the bar a few weeks back it had been a whirlwind of passion. Gary had never met a girl like Hannah before. It sounded cliché, but usually any woman he met in a bar was as smart as anyone was after a few drinks, and just as obnoxious. But Hannah was different, she was smart as a whip, came across as very cultured and Gary felt she challenged him as well as held his interest. However it wasn't the deep meaningful conversations they had which made them keep coming back to each other. They would meet, try and be adults and invariably erupt in a sexual melee that would last the weekend.

Something troubled Gary each time they met. While on the outside she was immaculate, there always seemed to be something worrying her, making her look over her shoulder and hope that someone or something wasn't there. He would try asking her about it, but she would wave him off and distract him with drinks or her feminine wiles. He had tried enquiring about her life every morning they woke, but each time she just gave him a sly grin that masked the concern her eyes betrayed.

This time would be different though. As Gary held her and kissed her lips, he looked in her eyes and spoke softly to her.

"There's always a part of you that's so afraid, why?" he whispered, stroking her face affectionately to try and put her at ease.

Surprisingly, it did, and Hannah began speaking of another man, her husband. She spoke of the usual things: how he didn't love her, didn't respect her, was cheating on her as well. Gary understood, he had had his fair share of one night stands with married women, but there was something more to Hannah's story than a bored housewife.

He asked again, and Hannah became more reluctant. She tried doing the usual tricks of getting more intimate or slinking off in the nude to try and trick his mind, but Gary had begun to care about this woman. He wanted to know how bad it all was. He wanted to play the hero.

It was then that Hannah revealed everything to him. Her husband wasn't any ordinary everyman. He was Adam Norris, an infamous criminal who you read about in the news. Gary had read the name in the usual red-tops, about how Norris was a practitioner of the 'old school' of crime. An almost caricature of the days of the Kray's or Capone. An East End wannabe who had established enough of an empire to have an aura of legitimacy. The man was rightly feared, and it made sense why. Behind the veneer of sexuality that Hannah had, she always seemed terrified of her encounters with Gary.

Gary though, despite his humble trappings, still yearned to be the hero. He couldn't help it, as when the tears flowed down Hannah's cheeks he felt his heart break and every impulse in his body cry to do something.

He took her in his arms, stronger and firmer than before, and as their naked bodies squeezed together he looked into Hannah's eyes and uttered the words he'd soon regret.

"I'll protect you."

As the chill went through him, Gary sat cross legged in the middle of the cage. Some birds had flown over and began to peck away at the vomit that stained the bars in front of him. At first he had tried shooing them away, as every time they landed the cage would tilt and creak a little bit, stopping his heart a little bit more. But then with each wave of the arm the cage would sway again and before long Gary realized he was fighting a losing battle. The birds kept landing, the cage would move back and forth, and Gary would watch them as they feasted.

He would have felt hungry himself, if his mind wasn't fixated on his prison in the sky. Even as he sat there, barely moving a muscle, he didn't feel safe. His mind screamed at him many paranoid thoughts. The floor was weak and would collapse, the chain above his head would snap, the bars couldn't support his weight and would bend and break. Each fear resulted in the same grim prophecy: his body falling to the ground below. As it entered his mind Gary felt his throat gag and his eyes sting, not with cold but with the fear of a child. He didn't know whether his shaking was due to the cold or the terror.

He didn't have to think long before the distraction of the phone rang out. Gary felt himself jump, but he controlled it enough not to rock the cage. Slowly, he edged his hand into his pocket and produced the phone.

On the other end was the orchestrator of this whole ordeal, Norris.

"How's the view up there?" he asked, a sick chuckle punctuating the question.

Gary didn't answer, just listening as the old man continued to mock and berate him, calling him rude for not facing him, a coward for not getting up, the usual jabs.

Eventually he got to his point, probably the point he's been eager to make all along, Gary thought.

"Where is my money?"

"I don't know," Gary said, trying not to let his voice break.

There was a brief silence, neither man wanting to carry on the subject.

"You're lying to me."

"No I'm not."

"Hmm. Well, why don't we let you sit there and see if you can remember. I've got all the time in the world."

The phone didn't cut off, Gary assumed that Norris was waiting for him to either break down or give him a response that would allow him to goad him some more. Instead he just listened until he heard the old man snort and put the phone down. Gary had no idea if he was stood there watching him, waiting for him to dial back and cry for mercy. He just sat there, watching the birds, watching the horizon, and thinking about how the Hell he could possibly get out of this.

Then it hit him. He had the phone that Norris had given him. In a moment of fervour he grabbed at the device, momentarily forgetting it was already in his hand. For Gary it all seemed to happen in slow motion, as he saw his fingers fumble at the phone as it slipped out of his hands and bounced off the floor of the cage. He felt himself hold his breath as he watched helplessly as it slid close to the edge, gliding through the bars that separated him from Death. It didn't fall though, instead settling halfway between the steel and a sheer drop. As every nerve tensed in his body, Gary reached for it and felt the cage lurch with him. He could only watch again as the floor tilted and the phone made it's final movement off into the big empty below, Gary's outstretched hand maybe only inches away that seemed like miles.

It was when the momentum made the cage go at an angle that Gary snapped back into the now. In his desperation he had forgotten himself and now found he was stumbling toward the bars of the cage. As he tripped, he felt his face slam against the cold metal and his eyes being introduced to his potential fate. The air seemed to disappear from his lungs as he watched the phone plummet, and his body feeling like it was being pulled down with it. He found himself paralysed with fear, but with every second he looked down the worse he got. The birds around him were crying, his heart was thumping out of his chest, and all he could do was consider the very worst.

Eventually Gary put a foot back and found the cage hitting an equilibrium. He was on a level field again, and found himself collapsing once more onto the cage floor. This time though, he truly was alone, and feared not only the drop, but how Norris would respond.

Since discovering who her other half was, the element of danger in Gary and Hannah's relationship was never in doubt, but what she was now suggesting would take it to the next level of risk.

His protection was given a very simple goal: escape. Hannah no longer wanted to be under Norris' grasp and in Gary she saw someone who would help her get out of it. When they talked about the scenarios where this could occur, she wooed him with words and compliments and puppy dog eyes tainted with withheld tears. She spoke not of their lust, but of their love and future together. Their affair had been going on for a few months now and the emotions were still burning strong. This was to be the next step, she said, the moment where they would take the plunge.

Of course, what Hannah needed to escape, to escape with Gary, was money. Primarily, Norris' money. She told Gary how he wouldn't miss a few zero's here and there, and using his knowledge of computer systems acquiring it would be easy. She'd give him the details he'd need and all he'd have to do was the technical work.

For Gary, the pressure was now as intense as the passion. This was now the catch he had been waiting for all along. A pretty girl didn't fall into your bed without certain strings attached, and Hannah didn't have strings but razor-wire that would cut deep if you made a mistake. He had been feeling paranoid over their encounters since he learnt about Norris, and the idea of stealing from a man such as him would definitely up the ante. However, when he looked at her at night, as they lay with each other, he felt his heart scream over his head. He truly loved her now, and felt a need to take away from a life of abuse and hurt, and to something simpler. Something he could offer.

After she gave him the details it had been easy. Far too easy in fact. Using a few tricks some of the boys down at the office had taught him he managed to access Norris' account and moved a few numbers over to one that he and Hannah had set up together. With a bit of data manipulation, he fudged the records so nothing could be tracked back to them and even if in the worst case scenario, the amount was so minor in the grand scheme of things that several explanations could be given. A glitch, a lost expense, a drunken night out.

Afterwards, as they celebrated a bit too wildly, Gary felt the pain of paranoia start to sting his mind. All the doubts and anxieties flooded in and violently shouted at him. They asked questions he didn't want to consider: could he trust Hannah? Is he being set up? What happens if Norris finds out? He approached the window of the hotel they were in and thought he saw a familiar car parked outside, watching and waiting for him. He began to feel the pressure again before turning around to see Hannah beckoning him towards her, and feeling it all drift away again.

As the day turned to evening, so did the winds get stronger and more bitter. The cage rocked menacingly as the same paranoid thoughts returned to haunt Gary as he sat there. After losing the phone and not hearing from Norris, who was most likely spitting his name now, all he could do was think. The thoughts were all the same, telling him how he had made a huge mistake and this was his punishment, how he had played the wrong cards, got with the wrong woman and ultimately done the wrong thing.

This cage was his prison, and his sentence was to be death. There was no other way. Part of his mind, strangely in Norris' voice, condemned him as a fool. Since that night he had rarely spoken with Hannah, despite many phone calls and texts. Eventually she had contacted him and explained how Norris was suspicious and they needed some time apart before spending their life together. Gary had been trusting, as he had throughout, but as he sat there shivering he felt furious at his own stupidity.

His mind told him everything he feared, that she was too good for him, completely out of his league. That she had used him to get what she wanted, which was Norris' money. Hell, there was the possibility that they were in it together. Some sort of weird game they both played to get a thrill out of destroying a common man. People in high positions go to extreme places to achieve the highs that most people get out of a winning scratch card. People like Gary weren't just other people; they were toys to play with, to taunt and tease and torture. Yes, he had some of the best sex of his life, but most likely he was just a plaything for Hannah while they moved to this end game, where he sat like a bird in a cage, waiting to die.

Gary thought of what happened after he last spoke to her, how every shadow was watching him, every car filled with hoods and every message was a threat. For weeks he began to feel sick with worry, thinking things would catch up and spiral out of control but then... nothing. He felt himself begin to relax, to enjoy himself once again. His friends had helped him, taken his mind of things and soon Gary began to feel like the man of old, the man who he was before he had met Hannah. Yes it was boring and lacked the zest a woman like her gave, especially with the gangster husband and thousands of pounds they stole, but soon they melted into the past.

Then of course he found himself here, and all the horror came flooding back.

He was beginning to feel his stomach tighten with hunger, and his mouth dry up as he kept swallowing saliva to try and quench his thirst. Time had no meaning anymore up in the sky, only watching the clouds drift beside him and the sun arc it's way from one side to the other. In fact as Gary sat there, he found himself watching it as it made it's final descent into the horizon. Once it would go, he knew that the shivers would get worse, that the wind would become more of an enemy and that he'd probably die of hypothermia or something. Now he had no means of communication, Norris would have most likely given him up to die, waiting until the next day to get him down. If Gary was still breathing, he'd be dead anyway. There was no way he would be coming out of this now.

Instead, Gary just felt his mind start to give way, and his eyes fall heavy. He felt weak, tired, and ready for whatever was coming. Strangely, he had begun to accept his fate and was feeling calm about it.

He shut his eyes, and listened to the wind whistle and the cage creak with it.

With a start Gary woke up. It was dusk but there was still enough light to make out his surroundings, not that he could ever forget them. His skin was covered in goosebumps and he felt his fingers and toes clench in the cold, but that wasn't what woke him. What woke him was the sound of the crane.

It was alive, whirring and creaking and groaning at him as he sat there. For a moment Gary was confused, his head looking around for something he didn't know. Eventually he looked over at the booth of the tower crane. There was someone there, two people in fact. One person at the controls and...

Hannah.

Or at least he thought it may be. At this point part of him was thinking he was dreaming. Having some deluded fantasy where everything would come together. It wasn't until his brain registered the flashing blue light that was illuminating the crates below him that he realized that against all odds, he was being saved.

The crane itself kept creaking and crunching, promising movement. In his mania, Gary felt himself get up on his feet for the first time and stumble slightly, pins and needles crippling him somewhat. He held onto the bars to steady himself and felt elation break across his face. A long smile and a heartbeat told him that not only was he still alive, not only was this nightmare about to end, but Hannah had come back. She had kept her promise, they were going to be together.

Gary felt himself begin to get impatient as he listened for something that would say that he was going to be put back on ground firmer than a thin steel floor. In a panic, he began to wonder where he'd be put, before recalling the rooftop where Norris had been coldly watching him.

If the police were here, and Hannah was here to save him, then surely that meant as well that Norris was taken down. He went through scenarios in his mind where this could be possible, wondering if Norris had found Hannah and threatened her, only to overplay his hand. Perhaps the police had a sting in place and his situation was just a frightening tangent to their investigation. Either way, none of it really mattered, because all it did was give him the hope that he was going to be released.

Eventually, there was a hint of movement. The crane slowly drifted to the left, away from the rooftop where Gary thought he would go. He felt his heart pound through his chest as it stopped again. He then felt it nearly burst when the chain holding the cage dropped slightly, and suddenly, and Gary felt the first real feeling of falling. It was only a couple of feet, but it was so sudden that fear rushed through him. When the chain jerked taut, he felt that the force of his body would punch a hole in the floor and keep him heading South. Thankfully it didn't, and all the cage did was sway.

Then came the beginning of the end of his confinement, as finally the crane lurched the cage to the right, towards the rooftop. Gary steadied himself in the middle as the cage tilted more and more as the crane's arm sped up as it carried him. It wasn't fast, but it wasn't gentle, keeping Gary at an angle he wasn't comfortable with. But he wasn't thinking about angles, or speed, or the ever increasing darkness. He was thinking about falling into bed with Hannah again and crying with joy that they would once again be together. This time forever.

As these thoughts warmed him, the crane suddenly jerked to a standstill. In a moment, Gary felt himself lose his footing and fall hard against the cage and then... nothing. All he heard in that instance was metal crash against metal as he watched the floor of the cage tip badly against his stumbling feet. He felt the traction he once had slip away and air hit him even harder than before. Instinctively, he felt his arms flail out and his hands grab painfully for anything it could and soon Gary found himself clinging for his life as he hung from the door of the cage.

He couldn't hear the cries from the control booth, or the gasps below him, all Gary could hear was his heart thump and the wind mock all around him. His fingers, numb and angry from the cold, nevertheless kept a firm grip and Gary managed to link an arm through the bars. But when the cage started slowly moving once more he found his body pulling him down. The door of the cage strained against the pressure of his weight and the wind stabbed at his fingers, threatening to make that grip disappear.

All Gary could think of was not of the door or the wind or the drop, but that Hannah would be there waiting for him. All he had to do now was hold on.

Sense

III

(dead)
(I'm dead)
(I have to be)
(because)
(because this)
(this is hell)
(one day)
(I was walking)
(next day)
(I'm here)
(dark room)
(bright light)
(and someone)
(something)
(against me)
(spoke a lot)
(now nothing)
(I think)
(I think)
(he's dead)
(dead as well)
(we're all dead)
(all dead)
(because)

(because this)
(this isn't life)
(this is torture)
(this is nightmare)
(this is hell)
(I'm dead)
(I'm dead)
(I have to be)

IV

What do you see?

(I don't know)

What do you see?

(I don't know)

Do you see anything?

(I don't know)

Do you see visions?

(I don't know)

Do you see shapes?

(what he wants)

Do you see

(I don't know)

Colours?

(I don't know)

People?

(why he does this)

Memories?

(I don't know)

Things?

(I don't know)

Anything?

(I don't know)

Anything at all?

(I don't know)

In there?

(I don't know)

In the light?

(anything anymore)

…

(I don't know)

OK

(I don't know)

Next time

(I don't know)

We'll try again

(I don't know)

The Legend of the Rogue

Well hello there weary traveller! Been on quite the journey have you? Oh yes, I can well imagine. I used to journey when I was a young buck like yourself, but then I had a rather unfortunate encounter with a whore from the lands of Braxia and, well, you've seen those Braxian women!

Anyhoo... can I get you something? Some Moon Juice perchance? Or maybe a bite of Lork Pie? It has fresh spreg in it! I would offer you a puff of my pipe, but it's filled with shreds from the Palah Plant, and will most likely melt the lungs of a first-timer like you!

Well, if I cannot offer you any of that, then I will offer you a tale to ease you into a state of utter relaxation! Don't look too wary, as it is of an adventurer much like yourself, who entered the lives of many a figure and left them with a memory of utter wonder and amazement. And a few holds in their back, but that was only the ones he didn't like.

I should start by confirming that it wasn't around these parts. No, the villages in the Derren District are quite peaceful and have no time for crazy people going round doing derring-do such as yourself! No, we are quite content spending our time with harvests and summer dances, and of course the odd hallucinogenic cocktail. One has to unwind somehow.

No, this tale took place in a far off land, you may have heard of it, called Covers Arc. You look confused! Well, Covers Arc is an island, quite a large one, probably the size of a small God. One of the Old Ones, like Ptyath. But with less stingy bits.

I digress. Covers Arc was rich with spirit and wealth and other such material delights that would boggle the simplest of farmer's minds. But, with all that gain, comes glory and the thirst for it. Various criminal enterprises and budding questers travelled far and wide across there, looking for a quick fortune and a quicker reputation. There was everything from Pirates to Orcs, Mages to Necromancers. It was most definitely not a place for the faint of heart!

Within those parts a man of any species could make his way in the world, and one made their way more than anyone else. His name was Lasombre, and that was all anyone really knew of him. He was aligned to no tribe, no enterprise, and no guild. He was a lone wolf, back before they were a thing. You've come across the Lone Wolves of Vahn? Course you have, those ironic bastards get everywhere. "Oh look how lone we are! In a pack. Of Wolves. Because we're Lone Wolves! Oooooh!"

Where was I? Oh yes, Lasombre. No, some wondered whether he was an Agent of the Gods, sent down to put us to task for our immoral ways and loss of heart. Others thought him sent from the very bowels of Hell, the really smelly parts. A vengeful spirit. Others of course said he was a spurned lover looking for his true, but that was just silly.

Lasombre came to Covers Arc already with quite the amount of weight behind his back. Bedecked in an armour that would stun the blind, full of sparkling gems and smooth steel. He wasn't flashy though, he just had a look that would stop you in your tracks and, if you were inclined, drop your pantaloons.

But the thing to watch for were the two blades he wielded. Now of course, you wouldn't see them before it was too late, but some lucky witnesses stated that they were made of a material never seen before by the eyes of mortals. Was it pure Onyx, taken from the very heart of a dragon? Or was it Bloodbone, the fabled skeleton of a Khad Imp. No-one really knew, but the stories spread regardless.

Before he had stepped onto the isle, he was already hired in the service of a Town-Master there named Dyan Makavill. Makavill, a mildly corrupt individual, wanted Lasombre to... 'remove' a rival of his. However he had taken the rogue for a thug, and Lasombre's beautiful way with words and wisdom beyond his years stunned the oafish Town-Master. Nevertheless, after much negotiation Lasombre took the quest, given his honour to those that granted him work.

But of course, Makavill was a cunning beast, and lore goes that when Lasombre arrived to perform the deed, assassinating an elf by the name of Leaph Sarray, he instead found Sarray and his family pre-slaughtered, and a council of Guardians on their way to arrest the rogue in the act.

Naturally, when Makavill was bought to the scene, he found his loyal Guardians in a worst state that the butchered Sarray. Some say it was difficult to connect one body part to another!

This put Makavill in a state of extreme terror, and he made sure that his chambers were guarded day and night, from the early dawn to the darkest dusk. Eventually it came to a time when no-one entered, and Makavill himself never left. His guards would check on him, finding the Town-Master in a constant state of anticipation for the day vengeance would come.

And one day, it did. Makavill was found in his bed with more holes in him than Faqen Cheese. There was no sign of any forced entry, nor any disturbances and most of all, Lasombre. He had appeared to do his duty as silently as the wind blows, but with more ferocity.

A number of years passed before anyone really spoke of Lasombre in grander terms. Yes, a few minor farmers and peasants spoke of a rogue who would help them in a way just and true, but no-one in the higher echelons ever spoke of him.

That was until the day he found Paobert Kevund. And history began.

You see, Covers Arc had fallen into deeper corruption after the death of Makavill. The High Priest who ruled the land had decided that the best way to quell the common folk was through hardship and brutality. Through fear, no-one like Lasombre would dare launch an attack unless they wanted the people to suffer as a result. Budding heroes were cut down in their path and paraded in their death throes for the so-called 'awe' of the crowd. An iron grip swept the land like a disease. Darkness fell upon Covers Arc.

But in darkness, the blackest of minds prosper, no matter how pure of heart they may well be. Paobert Kevund was slowly making himself known as a Berserker. He wielded a hammer and struck it with a ruthlessness and anger that even those he was in service to cowered before him. He was like no other Berserker seen before; pulverising and slight of mood, yet blessed with an intelligence that mystified those he spoke to. He was an out of control animal without focus, until Lasombre found him.

The two of them found a peace within each other. Kevund found a comrade who would bring solace to his most brutal of times, while Lasombre had something he hadn't anticipated requiring; a brother in arms. Together, the two of them unleashed themselves onto Covers Arc, righting wrongs and helping villages and townships recover from the tyranny of the High Priest's reign.

It all culminated when the two arrived in the City of Iua, where the High Priest resided. He threw waves of men to fortify the city walls and to protect only those who earned his favour, dignitaries and money-men who protected his tainted wealth. However, as he watched from his tower he could only shiver as he saw Kevund throw his men around like small animals, and Lasombre dice the others like soft bread. The two warriors fought as their styles dictated; Kevund was hard and fast while Lasombre was swift and unseen, but both were without mercy. But what the people spoke of afterwards was no matter how violent their attacks, not a hair was harmed on the innocent.

When they reached the High Priest, he begged mercy on the names of the Gods. He spoke of untold riches that would be granted to the men should they let him live and join their side, and how they were to become beings of a status never before known.

When the people saw their High Priest naked and carefully navigating the thin, gusty highs of the City's cloud structures, they knew their two heroes had made the right choice.

So you wonder, did Lasombre and Kevund rule over the City now the High Priest was gone? My friend, you misjudge the character of these true champions of the masses. They left the City of Iua to those honest and kind, but with a warning that should that ever change, they would return to set things right. The City of Iua and Covers Arc as a whole prospered under the new rule, and Lasombre and Kevund made sure it remained that way for a few years.

However, all good things must pass, and soon Lasombre and Kevund found themselves going on separate paths. The two would forever be in each others hearts, not as comrades but as brothers, their bond stronger than any Iron a blacksmith could forge. Kevund travelled to the Valleys of Tywah, taking on mythical beasts for sport while satisfying his appetite for mead and female folk.

Lasombre however was of more humble tastes. Those who studied him at the time say he returned to his home-land, wherever that may be, and settled down with a fair maiden who like him, was skilled in the art of battle. Together they fought foes and aided those who required it. And in love, they were as strong as they were in battle. Some say they joined a guild where their quests bought them much glory, and the world much peace. Others say Lasombre settled down and became a farmer, crafting the most glorious spices a mortal could taste.

But in some dark corners, where the nefarious and dark of spirit reside, rumours still abound that Lasombre will come back, with his maiden and his brother Kevund in tow, to cease any depravity or callousness that is being practiced. Others say he already has, and not lost a step, riding the wind like a leaf and striking with as much pain as an arrow.

Now, those are just stories, and far longer than the one I have told you this eve. You need to sleep! For to even begin to match the standards that Lasombre reached, you require a lot of strength, a lot of stamina, and a lot of honour in your heart. If Lasombre and those that walk with him have taught us anything, it's that blades and blood can get you so far, but a mind sharp as any dagger, and integrity as strong as any armour, will always win whatever challenge you face.

What's that? You're already asleep! I've been talking to myself? Well that makes sense; this Palah Plant is strong stuff. I'm not even sure you're real. You could even be a Rat-Weasel nibbling away at my toes. No matter, another smoke and I shall be far and away in the realm of dreams. Of warriors true and rogues that defy their very name with their righteousness...

Sanctuary

It was close to 10 as the Father made his way around his quarters to perform his nightly checks. Making sure the lights were out, the windows were closed and other small tasks that the average person would surely find dull, but for him were now routine. His modest living space was part of the Church. Here, he did his part in spreading the message of the Lord, and much like where he lay his head, his task was not great, but important. The town where he was based was quaint, as visitors would say when they visited, and the Church formed an important part of it. Father would not dare say he was proud, per se, of how he handled the place of worship, but he took great solace in what he did manage to do.

He made his way into the main part of the Church, and looked down the nave toward the great stained glass window before him. The light from the street lamps outside illuminated the interior like the few candles never could, filling them with a multi-coloured glow from the series of visions surrounding him. It was always the main window, above the altar, which filled Father with fervour though. He would look at Jesus standing there, tall and powerful and forgiving, and be glad to be under the love of such a being. Every night he would take in these holy visions, and let them help him sleep into the next morning.

Father reached his room, set his water on the side and made his way into bed, puffing out his candle before resting his head. Tomorrow was another day, and as always he looked forward to it. He closed his eyes, and began to relax.

A loud hammering shook him from his rest. Each blow reverberated through the Church's walls as if the door itself was being smashed down. Father looked at his clock and saw the hands telling him it was near after 2. Slowly, he gathered his senses and made his way toward the main aisle.

Wounded by sleep, he slowly made his way to the solid wooden double doors that gave entry to the atrium of the Church. With each step he took, the banging from outside grew in ferocity and repetition. It wasn't until he was a few feet away that he suddenly heard the word that chilled his bones.

"Sanctuary!"

With the blood pumping fiercely in his heart, Father fumbled the key from his pocket and widened his eyes to awaken himself some more. He put the key in the lock and turned, the door giving way with a brief *click*.

For a moment there was nothing but silence. Before Father could react, the door swung hard against him and in fell a young man, dressed head to toe in black. He fell to the ground, on his hands and knees, and looked up with fear at Father.

"Sanctuary." he whispered again.

His eyes were begging to Father, before they darted back beyond the door to the grounds outside. For a moment Father was curious as to what he was looking for before the young man bounded up and slammed the door shut, resting against it.

Both men stood there in silence for a moment, Father stood looking at the young man before him, while he leaned gasping against the door. He paused, turned to Father and implored him to lock the door. When Father asked why, he answered simply.

"I asked for sanctuary, for that I need a locked door."

The young man smiled at the confused Father, and laughed breathlessly as he introduced himself as John.

"Well John," Father said as he locked the door, "you look like you could do with a cup of tea."

Father led John back down the nave toward his quarters, and watched as he slowly walked down toward the altar, taking in the glass visions of the Lord around him. The colours basked them in a holy glow, aided by the streetlights outside.

John drank his first cup quickly, in spite of the heat, and seemed to relax. When troubled souls had come to Father, he had always found a cup of Earl Grey to be the finest thing to get them in a state of wellbeing. Most came in fear of the Church and what it represented, so to get them to unburden themselves Father felt you had to put them at ease first and show them that God wasn't all sin and judgement. The young man known as John didn't seem as troubled now that he was inside, but still looked to the door a number of times to check that nothing was coming for him.

Father started as softly as he always did, by asking about John. The young man wasn't too forthcoming with details, save a reiteration of his name and his status as a visitor to their town. Father noted his dress in more detail, a fine combination of well kept shirt and trousers, with an obscenely polished pair of shoes upon his feet. All in the deepest black.

Father noted this to John, who smiled fully for the first time and jested about Father's observation.

"I never put a vicar for a fashion expert."

Father smiled softly back and decided to broach the subject of John's troubles. Why had he come in such a panic? John asked to pour himself a cup of tea, and spoke as he filled his cup. He had arrived in the town a couple of days prior, on business, and had taken to seeing the sights of what there was to offer, which was not much. Therefore, when not conducting his work, he took to one of the oldest vices there was, the various public houses around. John explained to Father that the first night he drank a great deal and made several friends, sharing amusing tales and listening to their problems. John explained he was a good listener, and, while not being arrogant in his assumption, was very good at giving advice to those who needed it. With a nod, Father told him that was a trait they shared.

John continued to tell how he met a girl, and Father began to see the pieces fall into place. John said how he and the girl got along, shared some laughs and of course, some drinks, and eventually, well, as John put it:

"We did what young people do when they've had quite a few drinks."

He continued that the next night, after conducting his business, he once again drank, discussed and divulged in carnal relations with the same girl. Nothing untoward and definitely, as John was at pains to point out, nothing of an ill nature. However John explained that this, the third night of his enjoyment of the town, he found himself confronted by the brother of the girl. He explained how the brother was unhappy with John's involvement and when others came to his defence, the situation escalated to such as degree that violence was involved.

"The next thing I knew," John said, "I was running for my life."

Father nodded and then asked John what made him come to the Church? Why not the police or one of his new found friends?

John considered this for a moment and then answered.

"I've always found comfort, in the Church."

He then explained what the lost art of 'sanctuary' meant; unlike, say, a police station or person's home, he knew he could not be turned away.

"And sure enough," he finished, "here I am. Safe and sound."

Father took all this in and began to form his council in his head. He had heard of many young folk who indulge in vices only to then have anger erupt before them. He asked John to answer truthfully if he had done anything that could be construed as "bad", to which John asked back a simple question.

"What's bad?"

Father tried explaining that some of his actions, especially to the girl's brother, may be seen as disrespectful or even uncouth, to which John again asserted he had been nothing but a gentleman and had done nothing untoward.

Before Father could enquire more, another series of knocks rattled across his door.

Father made his way back down to the doors, leaving John in the safety of his quarters with another cup of tea. As he opened the door this time, there was no-one falling through his door, just a group of people all looking rather concerned at him.

Father looked at them all and their expressions, twisted with anger and fear and other ugly emotions. He asked the man leading them who had knocked on his door, and what they wanted. Although he already knew what it was to be.

The man, who Father concluded was the brother in question, spoke about John in vile terms. He spoke of how the young man had not only defiled his younger sister, but also poisoned her mind and those around her. Father asked how this could be, and a lady behind him shouted passionately about how John had convinced her husband to leave her. Another spoke about how he had turned their children against them and before long the chorus began singing the same tune. It was one filled with rebellion, with spite and conflict, and all by John's hand.

For a moment, Father struggled to take all this in and once again asked if John had done anything that really necessitated such an angry mob. The Brother spoke up again, talking more of John's way with words and his corruption of his young sibling.

"She's only 17 Father, still a child, and he has stained her physically and mentally."

While these words chilled Father, nevertheless he informed the group that the young man by the name of John was under his protection for the moment. Father spoke of how he feared that the group would do something rash, something drastic, something violent. He reminded them that revenge was not a path to take, and in fact was a path that would stain them all for a lifetime.

For a moment the group, especially the Brother, would not move, but their heads bowed as if Father's words had stuck with them. From the back, they started away but before they left the Brother looked at Father solemnly.

"He's bad news Father. He's toxic."

With that, the Brother turned away sadly and made his way down the grounds, leaving Father to close the door once more.

Father returned to find John had started reading the Bible, although he could not make out which part before John closed it shut. He looked up at Father curiously, keenly aware of who had been at the door. Father took his seat and poured a cup of tea, before mentioning that the girl John had spoken of was only 17. John didn't react, or at least not how Father had hoped, instead claiming ignorance on the fact. He explained that as far as she had told him, she was of age. And besides, in his defense, she was not of an *illegal* age and had, indeed, consented.

Father then brought up the subject of the 'poisonous words' that the group had said John had spoken to their loved ones. With a sudden bellow that made Father's heart stop for a moment, the young man laughed heartily and smiled widely. He explained that those he had drank with and befriended all had troubles that needed directing, and that he had given the best directions he could. Naturally, he concluded, those directions would not please those who had caused the troubles. Father responded by asking that surely the best advice would be for the best of both parties, but John argued otherwise.

"What if one party is wrong? Seriously wrong?"

Father argued that it is not for one person to judge, to which John silently took on board. Father asked John if any of his 'advice' had been negatory in nature. John asked what he meant, and Father asked whether any of John's words had provoked a reaction that may lead to terrible actions. Again, John asked for clarification of what Father meant and the aged vicar struggled to find the words. John asked if he meant that he encouraged these people to commit adultery, violence, worse? Father didn't answer, but John did for him.

"I'm not responsible for how people interpret what I say."

John explained to Father that each person was their own, and that his words were merely noise in a larger chorus. He compared it to how some people with a musical ear will hear the rhythms of the guitar, the beat of a drum or even the lyrical quality within a persons voice. In the end, John concluded, what a person takes away from it is what's inside themselves.

"But surely morality will guide them," Father said.

"Depends on what you see as morality," John retorted.

Father could feel himself getting into a debate, but could not help himself into entering it. Many a time the souls who found their way here were non-believers, or worse fervent atheists who would spit in the face of a man speaking gospel to them. But Father felt John was different, wiser perhaps, and knew he would have quite the debate.

Father laid out his ideas of morality, of doing good to your fellow man, of helping and aiding and doing what's right for the betterment of everyone. John sat back and asked if all men followed this particular path. Father knew not every man did, but the majority had a moral compass that would show them the difference between wrong and right. But John then asked, to what degree? What if, in helping one, he was hurting another?. He bought up the theory of a Sophie's Choice, to which Father responded that such a scenario, while dreadful, was not a common occurrence. John disagreed, replying that degrees of morality were constantly battling with each other, and in fact during his nights here he had seen the waverings of right and wrong close at hand.

"My job means I have to see to what levels people operate, and I have to tell you that there are many shades of grey Father."

Father wanted to try and convince John otherwise, but was once again greeted by a knock at the doors of the Church. He excused himself once more, as John poured the last of the tea.

This time, Father was greeted by two very concerned looking police officers. They asked the rudimentary questions of Father's position and whether John was, indeed, inside. Father confirmed all this, and then asked his own rudimentary questions: Why were the police involved? Had John done anything illegal? And, in fact, was Father doing anything wrong in keeping him there?

The officers had no real warrant to storm in and take John, but began informing Father of the number of complaints that had been made against him. They spoke about how he had convinced one person to steal from their parents, told another to hurt his wife and, potentially, had raped a young girl. Father was taken back by these claims, but tried to maintain his composure. What evidence did they have of these claims? None, the police confirmed. Did the offenders in question confess, or even inform them of these claims. Especially the young girl. No, the police confirmed again.

"So why are you looking for this young man?" Father asked.

The police gave the stock answer of wanting to ask a few questions. With a weary sigh, Father understood and told them that he would send him to the station as soon as they'd finished talking themselves. The officers thanked him, and made their way.

"Be careful with him Father, some of the things they've said... well, just be careful."

Father smiled and waved the officers off, closing the door once more.

As he returned he found John taking in the stained glass window of Jesus standing before the altar. The street lamps illuminated the room with a predominantly dark glow and Father couldn't help notice how most of it faded around where John stood.

Without turning to face him, John spoke highly of the mural, and wondered aloud whether Jesus himself was a victim of his own morality. He helped people, he stated, and then found himself imprisoned and put to death for it.

Father asked, mostly in jest, if John was comparing himself to Jesus. But John just shook his head slowly and silently.

Father spoke again, saying that the police had called this time and spoke of grave scenarios. Of theft, violence and of most concern to Father, sexual violence. John finally turned to face him, his casual joviality gone and replaced with a grim stoicism. He questioned who had said such things, and Father confessed he didn't know. John again questioned the idea of morality and perception, and soon began to make the comparisons to the Son of God that he had denied previously.

Father felt himself getting very afraid of John now, as he stood before the altar with confidence and a voice full of weight. He came close to John and requested whether he could ask a simple question of him, to which John agreed.

"What, exactly, do you do?"

John paused before answering.

"I show people the truth."

Father looked at John, who had grown in stature before him, and saw his dark eyes look over his frailty. John spoke of whether the Father, in taking him in, in listening to his words, had broken any kind of morality. Father was shocked at this conclusion and denied it, but John carried on, stating how after everything he heard, Father had stood by

John and not given him up. Father again stated that John had come to him looking for sanctuary, that he had asked for his help, God's help, and he had provided him with it as asked.

John chuckled somewhat before saying that he never asked for God's help. Just Father's. And he had got it.

Father defended himself once more, saying that he had faith in John's side of the story. He spoke with conviction, that he had taken in poor souls before and tried to show them the right way. That, if John was indeed guilty of these crimes, he would convince him to do the right thing.

"And if I didn't, would you feel like you've failed?"

"Why, yes. Yes I suppose it would."

"So if I did you'd be proud?"

"Of you? Of course."

John just smiled at Father. He turned to the old man and began to speak firmly down to him. He told Father that if he had been wrong, and that he had helped him in spite of all the sin he had committed and asked him to justify with an idea of morality and pride at "doing the right thing", then surely he was as guilty as he was.

Father disagreed, and argued that he was providing the best counsel with the information John had provided him with. But John said that he had done the same with those around him previously and found himself pursued by people claiming he had done wrong. What if, John proposed, the people that Father had helped, that had felt pride in helping, had 'gone wrong' as well?

Father wanted to respond, but found himself lost for words. Instead John helped him, arguing that the Father had at first wanted to help those in the name of the Lord, but soon found himself drunk on the power of being the moral guardian. Instead of believing in the morality of the figure's surrounding him, brightened by the light outside, he had started believing his own gospel, reading from his own good book. In a sense, John argued, the Father had lost his faith in his God, and made himself his own.

"And yet still you stand here, trapped by a sense of duty you abandoned a long time ago."

Father felt tears fall from his eyes as he stood there, unable to speak. Instead John put a hand on Father's shoulder and whispered in his ear.

"You let the Devil in your home, forgetting that it's His. I don't think he'd forgive that."

And with that, Father was left alone before the altar, the multitude of hues from the glass visions around him darkening.

It was a bright day, and the park was full of life. Children played with their parents and each other, young lovers took each other in hand and smiled sweetly toward one another. It was a day that people would often praise the Lord for, both literally and figuratively.

For the Tramp once known as Father, it was a quiet place where he could sit on a bench and contemplate. Everything was confusing these days, so the noise of those around him helped drown out the questions that bogged his mind with venom. He had left the Church, left the town and left those who had taken his counsel and never looked back, instead taking to a life of homeless shelters and benches such as the one he was sat on. At night he found himself tortured, but during moments like this he suddenly felt at ease.

As people rushed past him, on their way to this place and that, he felt his eyes finally closing and not scaring him with dark thoughts. As he felt his head bow, one particular set of legs dressed in black that had paced past stood before him again. As the Tramp looked down, he couldn't help but notice the finely polished pair of shoes the person was wearing.

"You could do with a cup of tea."

The Tramp looked up and felt his eyes widen and breath quicken. John, or whatever his name really was, stood before him with a smile as wide as the horizon, and a large styrofoam cup of tea steaming in his hand. He handed it to the Tramp, but his grip had long since gone and the contents spilt to the floor. John's smile left, replaced by one of pity as he looked over the now shaking Tramp.

He took in his surroundings; all the happy people enjoying the green grass and bright skies. John nodded in delight, turning back to the Tramp. Once again, he put his hand on his shoulder, the Tramp flinching violently this time, and leant in close.

"Why are you so afraid old man? You're free."

With a quick pat, John, or the man who called himself John back when the Tramp called himself Father, briskly walked away. All he left behind was a terrified old man and a puddle of tea on the floor.

*feedthetroll

Doctors Notes:

The following were the last "chirps" written by Patient A from his online account. All sensitive information has been removed to protect those involved.

What we hope to gain from these are an understanding into the mental disintegration of Patient A. Currently they've shown extreme forms of Paranoia, Schizophrenia, Borderline Personality Disorder and general Delusional Behaviour bordering on the Psychotic. For historical purposes, the Patient was found wandering the streets, screaming at strangers about the information included within this document. Patient was then apprehended by police and bought to our attention.

Note: These "chirps" are only included for research purposes. They are not to be shared or distributed outside of these offices. Thank you.

If you'll bear with me a moment, I'd like to tell you a story. Hopefully, you'll listen.

It's about one guy who tries to save the world, even though the world doesn't know it.

And I'll warn you now, it doesn't have a happy ending.

I mean, to put in context, I'm typing these out in the rec room of a nuthouse.

It took a few months of convincing, but I got internet access. I plan to use it.

Anyway, I'm rambling. Background first.

Few years ago, a micro-blogging service called Chirp was launched.

I know, the very thing you're reading these Chirps on! *amazing

Anyway, it worked by allowing users to post messages of 100 characters.

It highlighted topics using something called "star-tags" *likethisone

And allowed you to communicate with others using by +ing them.

To most people in the early days, it was largely pointless and derivative.

At least, that was my early impressions.

After all social networking was a fad at the time, and this was the faddiest.

Early users didn't know how to use it, mostly posting the mundane and boring.

It ranged from "eating lunch" to "walking the dog".

However like most things of that ilk, it grew.

Celebrities started using it, thus making it cool.

From there other famous types, from porn stars to politicians, joined.

A Chirp-Chirp, or CC would grant you a unique window to fame.

People began to catch onto the cult of Chirp, and joined in 1000s.

Hell, some people even became famous from it, becoming Chirp-famous.

Anyway, that's how we got to the recent point.

Millions of people, Chirping in unison.

Like everyone else, I got sucked in and addicted.

While at times I'd try to be witty and get Chirpers, mostly I just vented.

I vented about life, about love, whatever was on my mind.

In a sense Chirp made me feel freer.

I met fellow Chirpers, found a little Chirp-fame, it was all quite cool.

Then one day someone CC'd something weird: *feedthetroll

Now understand, a lot of random star-tags appear on feeds.

Hell, I've seen some like *stuffmymommasaid and
*replacewordswithpasta

Humour is obviously subjective in the world of Chirp.

This one stood out though, for it's pure weirdness.

I asked the person who CC'd it why they did.

CC +(REDACTED) Because it seemed weird and funny

And it was, it was weird and funny and random.

I mean, *feedthetroll, what did it mean?

So I tried Chirping the original Chirper: +(REDACTED)

They didn't reply, so I left it at that.

Then I got a PM (private message) from +(REDACTED)

CC +(REDACTED) want 2 now abt *feedthetroll plz reply

So, naturally, I did.

Of course forgetting that curiosity killed the cat...

They explained that *feedthetroll was not a meme, but a warning.

Apparently, Chirp had a sordid side to it.

And I don't mean the random weirdo's who post crazy stuff.

Like this...

CC +(REDACTED) 45/m/Utah lookin for bearcub. Please + me.

I don't even know what a "bearcub" is...

Anyway, +(REDACTED) said Chirp was part of some sort of ritual.

Every Chirp was adding to power some sort of monster.

An "apocalyptic troll" who would end existence. Or something.

I know what you're thinking, another crazy Chirper.

I humoured them, it was the internet and I was bored...

They said everytime someone Chirped, the troll got stronger.

Everything from CC's, +'s, PM's... all fed the Troll

Apparently +(REDACTED) was part of a group who discovered this.

Conspiracy theory nuts who actually found something real.

They created the star-tag *feedthetroll as a way of spreading the word.

But +(REDACTED), who posted it first, vanished.

Trust me, I know how all this sounds...

Especially with the whole "troll" thing.

"Hey +(REDACTED)! Sounds like they're trolling you!"

I get that, I do, and I did at the time.

But like I said: Internet. Bored.

Anyway +(REDACTED) gave me a link to a site.

The site had pages of stuff about this, mostly rambling.

However they had recently acquired an address, a place for Chirp servers.

.+(REDACTED) was too scared to investigate, so asked me.

Well, it would get me out the house...

So they emailed me the info, and I went on a road trip.

Incidentally, I tried to PM +(REDACTED) again. Never replied.

Never Chirped again... *spooky

I got to the address, and it was the greyest building you saw.

A big box in the middle of an industrial estate. Anonymous.

I looked around for someone, but no-one home. No guards or anything.

So, I poked my nose in where it didn't belong, of course.

I snuck in through an open window, and found servers. Lots of servers.

So yeah, it's just servers. What you'd expect for a site like Chirp.

Giant cases, whirring away, all bedecked with the Chirp logo.

It was creepy, but largely troll-less.

Alas, as always with these things, curiosity got the better...

I wandered around the servers, alone. Seriously no-one about.

Then the smell hit me.

It was weak at first, but stank bad.

I must have been in a trance, as any idiot knows not to follow a smell that bad.

Jesus I was a fucking idiot...

I wish I hadn't done anything... just stayed out of it...

Fuck...

Anyway, I'm wasting Chirps.

That sounds funny when you read it back...

NO! STOP IT! FOCUS!

I followed the smell. It was bad, almost like toxic shit.

I followed it down some stairs, absolutely no light at all.

It took me a while to realize that the hum of the servers wasn't the only noise.

Like a low wheeze, was coming from the smell.

It was pitch black, so I used the torch on my mobile.

I went down the stairs, no idea how far down.

My phone's light cutting the black into shreds.

Then I saw it.

Well, I think I saw it... I saw something anyway.

When you say troll, you think a green goblin, like Shrek.

Or those little dolls you got as a kid with the big bright hair.

It wasn't like any of those. It wasn't like anything.

It looked a mess, like one of those morbidly obese people.

You know the ones that lie in bed and are moved by bulldozers.

It was like that, but covered in slime and shit.

I don't even know if it had arms or legs, it was just... a blob.

And it's face... well it wasn't a face.

It was all dark eyes and teeth. Bubbles of snot popping from somewhere.

I can't remember anything after that...

In fact my shrink, +(REDACTED) says it's a fantasy.

I got sectioned you see. They found me screaming in the street.

That was 6 months ago.

My doc, +(REDACTED), says I had a breakdown.

Chirp Addiction is what he called it.

I manifested some sort of weird story about *feedthetroll

Something to make the whole thing something... alive.

Something about removing the isolation factor. Or something.

But I have dreams... I see it there, in the dark.

I hear it wheezing, snorting those bubbles of crap.

And feeding off the words people Chirp, endless words.

It grows and bulges and infects everything like a fungus...

Apparently I had a moment where I wrote on the walls.

I lost my pen, which was annoying...

I tried telling +(REDACTED), but didn't listen.

Again, it was just "Chirp Addiction."

Maybe they're right, after all where am I now?

My purpose was to spread the word again, get someone else to stop it.

Burn the place down, break the site, something.

I don't know...

I just don't know anymore...

All I know is the compulsion, the need to Chirp.

To CC, to star-tag, to + Chirpers around the world.

To *feedthetroll

Like I am, even though I don't want to.

One day it'll have it's fill, and then what?

We become slaves, feeders, Chirpers.

Chirpers feeding a monster that will kill us all.

I honestly don't know anymore.

I don't know what to do anymore.

I don't know who I am anymore.

I'm now just a username.

I've failed. I couldn't win. Hopefully, if you're reading this, you might.

Spread the word. CC the Chirps. Meme the star-tag.

*feedthetroll

*feedthetroll

*feedthetroll

Ringside with the Kid

It had been a surprisingly warm February when his Dad presented him with two tickets to Wrestlerama's Inferno event, causing the Kid, a mere 8 years old, to lose control and run screaming around the house with joy. Wrestlerama was the big thing in wrestling, with a vast menagerie of colourful characters who beat each other up in the name of good and bad. Inferno was their main show, and it was coming to England as part of a World Tour. And now, finally, the Kid was going to be there too.

He had been a huge wrestling fan since he was old enough to look at a TV screen. One day he caught a brief glimpse of two men in bright trunks throwing themselves around a square ring tied together with three red, white and blue ropes. His parents had been channel hopping, but once the Kid saw the action they had no choice but to stop and watch.

It sucked him in immediately. While at first he didn't understand the intricacies of the stories, he recognised the good guys and the bad guys, and got excited by the thrill of the action that would take place. Big, burly men would smash, while smaller, more lithe athletes would use their speed to surprise. The Kid drank it all in and became more and more addicted as the years went on. He asked, and occasionally got, all the merchandise he could write down; T-shirts, action figures, videos and even comic books. The Kid owned them all and one of his proudest moments was unveiling his Killer Konrad T-shirt in the playground to impressed gasps.

Killer Konrad was one of his favourite wrestlers. He was a stocky, crew-cutted brawler who would pick up his opponents and slam them down to pin them. No-nonsense and tough, but always fought for the side of good. As well as him, the Kid loved the cowboy tag team of the Jenner Brothers, the scary Damien D'Ath and all-American hero JJ Cutter.

But as his Dad showed him the tickets for the Inferno event, the Kid saw his most favourite wrestler embossed on them: El Diablo, a Mexican luchador who's highflying antics left the Kid's jaw on the floor. Watching him bedecked in a Gold and Cream costume complete with a mask hiding his true identity was almost exhausting. The Kid would be in awe as he struggled to keep up with the variety of moves and attacks El Diablo would unleash upon his opponents.

The Kid hugged his Dad tightly. He expressed his gratitude so much, that his voice was hoarse before he went to bed the night before the event. After changing into his PJ's and brushing his teeth, his Dad tucked him in and ruffled his hair. He warned him that if he got too excited he'd end up staying awake, and fall asleep during all the matches. But the Kid was determined. He shook his head and vowed he would conk out as soon as his head would hit the pillow. His Dad just shook his head with a smile and kissed him on the cheek, wishing him sweet dreams and warning him of an early start.

Sure enough, as soon as the Kid's head hit the pillow... he was wide awake. He seemed to toss and turn for hours before finally finding himself in the ring, standing between El Diablo and the villainous Grand Titan, a mountain beast of a man. He was in referee's stripes, and was watching as both men collided in the centre of the ring. He watched blow after blow strike down on El Diablo, listening to the commentary unfold deep within the darkness surrounding them.

"By God! How is El Diablo gonna get out of this one Paul?"

"Put simply, he isn't! He's in 7 shades of Hell right now!"

The Kid watched as Grand Titan lifted El Diablo high up above his 7 feet frame, and threw him far out past the ring ropes.

"There is no way, guaranteed, he's surviving that one!"

"Somebody tell the ref to end this thing! Right now!"

The Kid saw himself standing there, paralysed as Grand Titan turned his attention to him and signalled for his finishing manoeuvre, the Titan Slam. The Kid could barely move as the giant began stalking him, slowly getting closer and closer until...

Until the crowd roared again and the Kid watched as El Diablo soared out of the darkness and landed with both feet onto Grand Titan's back.

"I cannot believe my eyes! El Diablo has hit Grand Titan with a stunning double dropkick!"

The Kid watched as Grand Titan fell and El Diablo jumped on top for the pin. He hit the mat three times and then the crowd roared again, El Diablo popping up and waving his arms. As the Kid stood there, he saw El Diablo turn to him and approach. As the masked luchador offered his hand, the Kid heard his Dad's voice.

"Come on Kid, time to wake up."

It was the morning of the event, and his Dad lifted the Kid's groggy body from the bed and carried him down the stairs to the cereal and cartoons that awaited him.

It seemed like forever until the moment came where the Kid was strapped into the back of his Dad's car, ready to leave for the Wrestlerama show. He watched impatiently as his Dad quickly headed back to the front door to say goodbye to his Mum, before heading back and jumping in the front seat. He turned back to the Kid and asked him if he was excited. The Kid nodded so much his neck began to hurt after.

They drove past houses and fields, through bigger roads and motorways, before they reached the big buildings that represented the City. The Kid craned his head, desperate to see if they were at their destination yet, his restraint fading fast the closer they got. It was only a few minutes later when the Kid looked out and saw the familiar giant arc of the Stadium where Wrestlerama Inferno was taking place. He squealed with glee, which earned a chuckle from Dad.

The Kid had never seen so many people in one place as they walked the short way to the arena section of the Stadium. They were all Wrestlerama fans as well, dressed in a uniform of bright T-shirts showcasing their favourite past and present wrestlers. The Kid recalled seeing people wearing the image of such greats as Cort Maverick and King Hurt, as well as the cool designs exhibiting the likes of Konrad and, of course, El Diablo.

Once they arrived at the arena there were queues so long the Kid began to worry that they'd never get in. That they had come so close but ultimately be turned away at the door, no doubt by the scary Grand Titan himself. He expressed these fears to his Dad, who simply laughed and claimed if that were the case, he'd take on Grand Titan himself.

The Kid thought this was stupid, as Grand Titan would destroy his Dad.

As they waited though, slowly the queue got closer and closer to the door, until eventually they were inside. The Kid gasped as he looked at all the banners displaying his favourite superstars, larger-than-life characters who were blown up to God-like proportions on posters hanging from the ceiling. He gripped his Dad's hand as he led him through the crowds, eventually getting to a thicker crowd of people all huddled up. His Dad lifted him up and showed the Kid where he'd taken him: the merchandise stand. He looked at his Dad, who told him he could have anything he wanted. Without even blinking, the Kid chose:

A T-shirt, with El Diablo jumping through the sky on it, and a replica gold and cream mask. Just like his hero.

Dad was more boring, just getting a program which he let the Kid read. Inside were all the stars, their stats and achievements thus far. The Kid regaled his Dad about how El Diablo had won the Light Heavyweight title from Damien D'ath, and was now looking to challenge for the World Title. He had just one obstacle.

Grand Titan.

Dad looked at his watch and told the Kid that the show would be starting soon. He picked up the Kid and carried him through to the main arena. It was everything the Kid had imagined, seats stretching up to the sky, circling a ring that looked 5 times as big as it did on TV. The Kid looked up at those who were sat in the high seats, so far away that any wrestlers would look like ants to them. For a moment the Kid was worried he would miss all the action, but his excitement grew more steadily as his Dad took him past each row of seats, until he was so close to the front he could leap over the barrier and tag team with the superstars himself.

A half hour passed, with the Kid talking nonstop about the history and stories so far. Dad listened intently, before pointing out the large screen where the wrestlers entrance was now on. The Kid was dumbstruck as highlight reels played, showing the amazing action he had seen on TV every week. And then just as he thought he couldn't get any more exhilarated, the lights went down and the show began.

For the Kid, it was almost all a blur. Pyro exploded so loud it made the Kid jump, reaching over to find his Dad already holding him. Then when the wrestlers came out the Kid couldn't believe how MASSIVE they were. They were as tall as trees and twice as thick in some cases. Killer Konrad, The Jenner Brothers, JJ Cutter, even a surprise appearance from Cort Maverick which got the crowd roaring with approval.

Then, at one stage, the Kid heard words which made him feel cold. Maverick, acting as the "booker" that night, said he was making the match everyone wanted to see.

"Tonight, to decide who'll face champion Johnny Patten for the World Title, El Diablo..." The Kid cheered along with crowd at the mention of his name. "... will face... Grand Titan!"

The Kid suddenly felt scared. He was shaking when his Dad put a hand on him and asked if he wanted to jump on his shoulders.

Sitting high up on his Dad, the world didn't seem so scary. The Kid was now at the wrestlers height, and felt confident enough to take on the world. He nearly fell off though when he heard the familiar Latin rock guitar of El Diablo's entrance.

There he was, exploding high in the air from the ground, pointing to the fans and running at such a speed the Kid thought it impossible. He was noticeably smaller than the rest of the wrestlers he had seen, but moved at a pace that made him seem invisible. The Kid watched as El Diablo leaped onto the turnbuckle, and motioned to all the fans cheering and chanting his name, the Kid included. He felt so buzzed that he almost didn't hear the CRASH of Grand Titan's music start.

As El Diablo warmed up in the ring, the Kid watched in stunned silence as Grand Titan walked slowly down the aisle. He wasn't just huge, he was the size of a house. His Dad, a strapping man himself, was a dwarf compared to Grand Titan, and the Kid suddenly found himself very frightened again.

He didn't want to watch when the bell rang, and Grand Titan began clubbing away at El Diablo, not giving a moment to run away. It was painful for the Kid to watch, reminding him of his dream where El Diablo was thrown about the ring like a rag doll. But just as Grand Titan was in control, he made a mistake and El Diablo slipped between his legs. The Kid watched in fervent glee as El Diablo hit swift kicks at the back of Grand Titan's knees, until he was down at his level. Then, the Kid almost wet himself with excitement as El Diablo ran at the opposite turnbuckle, seemed to glide across the ropes and leap off with a somersault over Grand Titan's head, grabbing his neck and hitting the sweetest neck-breaker the Kid had ever seen.

But it wasn't over yet. The Kid watched in anticipation as El Diablo went for a cover, and Grand Titan managed to throw him off at the 2 count. The audience around him seemed to "ooh" in agreement, and the Kid began to wonder if El Diablo was strong enough to take down the giant Titan.

El Diablo hit a few more kicks and elbows, before climbing the turnbuckle to launch one of his patented aerial assaults. The Kid was grinning hard as he watched El Diablo fly off... and land straight in Grand Titan's waiting arms. The Titan threw the luchador down on his knees once, twice, three times. Each successful blow reverberating through the Kid. He held on tight to his Dad's head as he sat on his shoulders, fingers digging deep into his Dad's scalp.

Titan started another crunching volley of clotheslines and slams, El Diablo becoming more and more limp with every successive fall to the mat. The Kid didn't know it, but tears were beginning to form in his eyes as he watched his hero be decimated at every turn. And then, the horror truly hit home. Grand Titan signalled for the Titan Slam. It was all over.

One of the Kid's hands hovered near his face, ready to cover his eyes as El Diablo would be slammed violently to the hard, uncaring mat. He didn't want to see it, but couldn't look away. He watched as Titan picked El Diablo up, the Mexican superstar barely able to stand, and thrust him up high into a press slam. The end was coming, and the Kid winced.

But then something happened, something so fast the Kid couldn't quite believe it. El Diablo pulled himself against one of Grand Titan's thick arms, swung round and wrapped his legs around the beasts head, spun round more for momentum and threw the giant to the floor with a devastating move known as a hurricanrana. The Kid couldn't quite believe it as he watched El Diablo stagger to his feet, look to the crowd, and point to the sky. The Kid was almost deafening himself with screams of joy as he saw El Diablo climb the turnbuckle, motion again to the skies, and fly off with a twisting corkscrew moonsault that seemed to defy gravity with each turn of El Diablo's body. He landed hard on Grand Titan, hooked his leg, and pinned him for the 1... 2... 3.

The place erupted, and no-one cheered louder than the Kid.

El Diablo celebrated in the ring, throwing his arms up in victory while his fast-paced music played. Soon, he left the ring and began high-fiving the fans next to the barrier. The Kid watched as his hero got closer, and closer, until he was eventually mere feet away from the Kid. For a moment, he watched as El Diablo walked past him, looked out pointing to the crowd, pointed at the Kid, and gave him a thumbs up. As El Diablo kept walking the crowd, the Kid felt himself bawling, not because he was sad, but because he was so happy. His Dad hoisted him off his shoulders and gave him a big hug. The Kid couldn't say thank you enough.

The rest of the show hardly mattered, but the Kid loved it all the same. After the main event and another "bonus match" featuring Killer Konrad team with Cort Maverick, the announcers told the crowd the show was over for now, but will be back next year and to get their tickets early. The Kid looked at his dad, his expression hidden by his replica mask. Dad just smiled and said maybe.

Outside, the air was cooler as night had descended over the City. The massive amount of people spilled out of the arena and headed towards their homes and transport, with the Kid and his Dad part of them. However, instead of going to where the car was, Dad was directing the Kid to the side of the arena. The Kid looked up and saw that his Dad had a mischievous look in his eye.

He noticed a few other fans had gathered to where his Dad was taking him, all brandishing notepads and pens. It took a moment before the Kid realized he was now at the wrestlers entrance, where they got into the arena.

They waited for a while before the first, low-card wrestlers emerged from the door. The fans around them, including the Kid's Dad, asked for autographs and some of the wrestlers duly obliged. Dad was using the program as a makeshift autograph book, and each wrestler was finding his profile and jotting down his signature. As each wrestler came out, their fame and stature grew. The Jenner Brothers, Damien D'Ath, even the terrifying Grand Titan emerged and gave his signature to the Kid's Dad. The Kid was shocked to see Grand Titan's hand was as big as his Dad's head. It was intimidating and even more so when Grand Titan saw the Kid in his El Diablo mask and growled.

But then, El Diablo himself appeared. The fans around him clambered for his autograph and the Mexican luchador obliged, scribbling his name across whatever they offered him. The Kid's Dad though, instead of offering his program picked up the Kid and held him before El Diablo. He shouted out that the Kid was a big fan, and El Diablo stopped and stood before them.

The Kid couldn't believe it when El Diablo held his hand out for a high five. The Kid obliged, and then watched as his Dad gave El Diablo a pen, and his hero signed the program, and then his mask. The pen tickled as it tracked across his head before El Diablo gave the pen back. Then the amazing happened for the Kid as El Diablo leaned in to talk to him.

"You're my hero..." the Kid whispered, his voice cracking with emotion.

"Gracias Amigo. Your Papi bring you tonight?"

The kid nodded, his lips trembling too much to talk.

"Then your Papi, he's the real hero eh?"

El Diablo stood up again, and offered one final thumbs up for the Kid before heading towards a waiting car. As the Kid watched him vanish into the night, he turned round into his Dad's arms and gave him the biggest squeeze he could muster.

And now, the Kid was the Man.

He always remembered that memory of meeting El Diablo fondly, and would tell his own kid's how amazing it was to be standing in the presence of not only a real superstar, but a real superhero. The Man would show them his signed mask, and tell them that El Diablo went on to win the World Title a number of times, and continue being the best until injuries got the better of him. The Man's kids weren't as interested in wrestling as much as him; the stories were too silly and characters not that interesting. But they watched the occasional main event and pay-per-view.

But the fondest part of the memory for the Man, the bit that he loved telling his kids most of all, were the ones that involved his Dad, their Granddad. He was gone now, taken while the Man was still a Kid. But with that memory of the wrestling, and all the other good ones that he held close to his heart, he would never be completely gone. The Man would remember those times, and feel the emotion well up as he thought about when he was ringside with his hero, his Dad.

The Dead Men

About 5 minutes walk from the Royal Victoria Country Park, commonly known as "Vicky Park" by the natives, Meg stood in the scraggly cluster of trees that stood for woodland. Armed with her trusty camcorder (the best that money could buy if you were an unemployed teenager), she was filming her friend Kay do her best zombie impression. And by best, she meant lurching around like a moron and making long, drawn-out groaning noises that quite frankly sounded stupid. But Meg wasn't a Romero just yet. She was barely a bargain basement Fulci.

"So why am I doing this again?" Kay asked, mid-groan.

"It's for a project."

"What project?"

"A zombie project!"

Kay mocked her with a handbagging motion and carried on her lurching and groaning. Meg's zombie project was, well, ill-defined. Like all film nerds, she had aspirations to make films and those aspirations mostly turned to zombie movies. Zombie movies were easy, cheap to make and most of all, fun. Everyone loved zombies. They were the cultural equivalent of toast.

So for the next five minutes she carried on filming Kay as she lumbered about the woods, occasionally pausing to bitch about having doing so. Meg jumped, twisted and turned to get all the angles; from the wide shots to the low angles, it would all be invaluable rushes for the inevitable masterpiece she would produce. Maybe. Depending if she could find other actors apart from Kay.

As she hopped around for another self-styled 'action shot', she saw something in the viewfinder. Emerging from the trees behind Kay were two men carrying some rather large bags. Kay saw Meg stop and, curious, turned to see what she was looking at.

Meg found herself feeling a tinge of embarrassment, she was always worried people would mock her attempts at being creative, but also a hint of fear. She had read a lot about having to have permits to film in public places, and was concerned that these two men, who looked a bit rough but still quite official, would tell her off. They definitely looked like park rangers, wearing dark green overalls over their clothing and badges hooked around their necks.

As they got closer, Meg found her heart beat fast. It wasn't helped when Kay decided to speak up.

"Could you hurry up please? You're in our shot," she asked sarcastically.

The younger of the two men, a gothic looking pipe hanging from his lips, looked at her, then at Meg with her camera, and the back at Kay. He stopped, the older man passing by, and removed the pipe so he could talk.

"Fuck off."

Kay's jaw almost fell to the floor as the younger man followed behind the older one again, heaving his large bag to his shoulder.

"You fuck off you prick!" Kay retorted.

The young man began to slow down, turning back to continue the verbal back and forth, but was called away by the older one. The two girls watched as they walked away toward the main park, the sound of muttering between them fading out as they went. Meg looked at Kay and could tell her back was up. She always got like that when dealing with confrontation. Sure enough, she turned to Meg and looked ready to punch someone.

"I need a drink, pub?"

They had been sneaking into the local pub for the past year now, despite both only being 17. How they succeeded where others had failed was simple: they kept their cool, knew how to act and dressed like the locals, a rag-tag group of alternatives, aging hippies and bear-like metal-heads with a penchant for black. They also avoided the alco-pops and instead drank the weakest cider the place offered, careful not to get drunk and stupid. It would usually take just two pints before they felt all dizzy anyway, so it was never a 'hardcore sesh', like some of the other underaged drinkers called it.

Kay, being the taller and thus older looking of the two, got the drinks and followed Meg as she escorted her outside. Their 'local', The Patterson Arms, was blessed with a big beer garden at the back, which was decorated by a cluster of trestle tables and a gazebo that was decorated with old comics and B-movie posters. It was this that appealed to Meg's inner geek, and thus became their hang-out point. If Kay's witterings about boys and the reality TV that was their fellow generation bored her, she could just read the comics and sit there nodding and agreeing.

The two girls had known each other since they were small 8 year olds. Once, Kay's mother had shown them a picture of way back in the day and it was horrifying to see them both so different to how they were now: Meg with her pigtails and ghastly braces, and Kay with her brutal pink dress. The pigtails and questionable fashion choices had since gone, but they had stayed strong friends, and it wasn't until recently that their paths had started to diverge. Meg was beginning to get heavily into her creative loves of film, film-making and anything else that defined her as a 'geek'. Kay though had begun to attract the attention of the male species, and had become quite addicted to the rush it gave her. It was as if they both knew that next year, when they left college, there was the chance they would finally separate and were preparing accordingly. It was one reason Meg was pushing to make the film, to have one final record of their friendship.

Sure enough though, as they sat there sipping their ciders Kay began telling Meg about a guy called James, some loudmouth emo kid from one of their English classes. Meg had always found him a bit full of himself and, at times, a bit of a bully. He was in a band, naturally, and had the ego to match, but zero humility. However Kay fawned over him, saying how 'mysterious' and 'clever' he was, while also noting how he had a great arse in skinny jeans. While expanding on this point, Meg was seeing how Captain America would defeat Nazi's this time. Or she would have, if something didn't catch her eye and make her spill her pint.

"What is it?" Kay asked.

Meg didn't answer, instead struggling to avert her eyes and hide her face behind whatever came to hand. The art of hiding yourself behind a semi-full pint glass or your own coat didn't scream subtle, so she instead just decided to lose all the cool she mustered and nervously ramble to Kay about Transformers.

Kay wasn't interested, instead she turned around and full-blown stared at the two men who had just entered the beer garden: the ones from the wood.

"Oh my fucking God!" Kay exclaimed. "What are they doing here?"

"Drinking?"

"Really?"

"Do the glasses in their hand not give it away?"

The two girls casually, as in not at all, watched the men make their way past and sit at a far table. Their bags and overalls had gone and instead they were dressed much like those around them. The older man had a greying Van Dyke beard and long ponytail, while dressed in one of those denim-vests with an eagle motif stitched into the back. The other one, who Kay called Mr Fuckoff, was younger, but with a larger beard and long hair held back by a bandana adorned with skulls. He looked more dapper, dressed in a suit jacket, but with clothing as dark as anyone around him.

"What do you think they're doing?" Kay asked.

"Will you stop with the stupid questions?"
"It's not a stupid question!"

"It's a stupid question! They're having a drink! Like we are?"

They carried on watching as the Mr Van Dyke Beard started rolling a cigarette while Mr Fuckoff produced his gothic pipe and lit it. They began talking, Mr VDB all smiles and theatrical gestures while Mr Fuckoff listened, nodded and then smiled the creepiest, widest smile Meg had ever seen.

"Do you think they're serial killers?"

"What are you talking about?"

"Well they had big bags before didn't they?"

"So?"
"So maybe... maybe they were getting rid of a body!"

"Don't be ridiculous..."

"Well they look creepy."

"They're the Dead Men."

Both girls looked round with a start to see Baker sitting next to them. He was a regular they had made the acquaintance of and all round cool nutter, all dreadlocks and crazy t-shirts. Today's said 'We're All Twats Here...' in white letters on a black background. Meg thought it was awesome, but then as Kay had told her, she was biased.

"What do you mean 'Dead Men'?" she asked.

Baker just shrugged. "That's what 5 Phone says. Spoke to them a few times. Decent couple of fella's."

He told them that the older one was called Winston van Huhn, and the younger Craig Vale. He explained that the legend went that they were grave-robbers, who spent the nights acquiring corpses for whoever had the cash to pay for them. The two were so good, they'd never been caught.

"That's creepy," Kay said, staring back at them.

"Tell them that," Baker smiled.

Meg found herself staring like a dope at Baker, and shook herself out of it by attempting some small talk on the decorations around them. But Kay was fascinated by the Dead Men, making comments about everything from their look to the way they were acting back to their supposed profession. Mostly everything ended with the same declaration.

"They're really weird."

Meg tried ignoring her, instead making several attempts to engage Baker in some sort of discussion. They had talked a few times and Baker had introduced her to several out-there films and publications as well as fuelling her desire for the independent scene. As well as other, unmentionable, things.

However, just as Baker was starting to listen to her attempts to sound cultured, Kay grabbed her arm and shook her violently.

"They looked at me!"

"So?"

"They know my face! They might be preparing to kill me!"

Meg looked over and sure enough, the Dead Men were giving the occasional glance to their table. However their looks suggested less murderous intent more gentle mockery. Vale would sneer a little while van Huhn would look over and begin making these zombie-like gestures. Both men would then laugh heartily. Meg felt a little hurt by it all and even more so when they both looked over and proceeded to wave sarcastically at them.

"I think we should go."

"Yeah, they're freaky."

"Ah don't go..." Baker said, extinguishing his fag before producing another. "Finish your drink at least."

"But they're taking the piss out of us."

"So what?"

"So it makes me feel shit."

"Why? You're cool."

And with that statement Meg found herself a little flush. She convinced Kay to stay to at least finish their drink and when that didn't fly, offered to buy her another. That seemed to work.

The three moved on from the Dead Men and began idly bantering, with Kay mostly holding court about how great James was. Baker livened things up by adding the occasional subtle remark that flew over Kay's head but made Meg laugh. They exchanged looks and Meg found herself looking slightly too long at Baker at times. She shook it off as a 'Silly Girl Thing'.

Halfway through a conversation about James band, Jubilant Mortuaries, Vale passed their table and offered an over-the-top salute which caught their attention and irked Kay. As he walked off, she turned to Meg.

"You should film them."
"What?"

"Film them! Like an investigation! Catch them in the act!"

"Why?"

"Well Baker here says they've never been caught grave-robbing, but we could catch them! We'd become heroes!"

"You've got a strange idea of what being a hero entails..." Baker commented.

Kay had a point though. Meg's creativity had been piqued by the thought of documenting the Dead Men. After all, she had many questions about what they did, and why. Were they a modern day Burke and Hare? And if so, how come they never got caught and who did they sell to? All these questions were enough to make her agree, although the cider probably didn't help.

Baker had the most sensible idea of the night though.

"I think you two girls have had enough. Let's get you home."

That evening, as the post-alcohol malaise set in, Meg found herself thinking more about what Kay had suggested. 'The Dead Men', as Baker had called them, would make an interesting subject, and a subject like grave robbing was morbid enough to gain people's interest. Your average Youtuber would jump at the chance to see something gross or horrible, the letters NSFW being a tantalising invite in the digital age.

As she recovered through several pints of water, Meg had a volley of text messages with Kay to try and convince her out that night. It was a

Saturday, and while their parents had forbidden any sort of 'partying' in order to 'protect a girl of her age', she was confident that she could sneak out, camera in hand.

Naturally, Kay was still as enthusiastic even though the drunken thrill had since worn off. A simple sneaking out later and the two were on course to meet up as the dusk settled in town.

Fitted with a fresh SD card, Meg filmed the crimson sky as she waited, the melting reds and oranges of the setting sun giving a nice ominous tone to the nights proceedings. Sat on a bench, Meg began her narration.

"As night settles on our sleepy town, darkness takes over. And nothing is so dark as to snatch the dead from their peace, their resting place. On this day, myself and comrade-in-arms Kay Butterworth will venture into a world that not only shocks us, but will shock you too. The world, of..."

"What you doing?"

Kay popped into shot and stared down the camera with her usual naïve chirpiness. Meg slammed the viewfinder shut and glared at her.

"You ruined my shot."

"You were just pointing at the sky!"

"I was building an atmosphere!"

Kay sneered. "Weirdo."

Meg ignored her and hopped up, careful to keep the camera in hand. She planned to keep it close in order to quickly snap anything interesting, or pick up some shots to throw in to bulk up the final edit. All the pro's do it, she was told by Baker, and so therefore she would to.

They began to wander down the high street, Kay full of pip and dizzy excitement. She began blathering on about The Dead Men, reinforcing her belief that they were "creepy" and probably "perverts or something like that." Meg tried not to listen until Kay bought up a very good point.

"So where exactly are we going?"

As the night began to creep across the sky, Meg stood there and thought. She had no clue. But she knew a man who did.

Luckily Baker was still in The Patterson Arms, a little more tipsy than before. Several empty glasses surrounded him as well as one glass half full with some tar-like liquid in it that made Meg grimace just to look at. He was surrounded by other alternative-looking types now, men adorned with tattoo's and piercings and women in corsets so tight it made Meg jealous, especially when they flaunted over Baker.

At first the girls had come unstuck. One of their pub rules was to enter before the door security got there, as gaining entry was much harder when you had some massive black-coat ID'ing everyone in sight. Luckily, they had mentioned Baker's name and he had vouched for them.

The pub was very different at night, a hive of flirtation, loud opinions and drunken laughter. A playlist of loud music assaulted the young girls' ears as the crowd seemed to revel in the chaos of it all. Baker was flitting between a conversation about monkeys with some girl whose boobs were about to explode out of her top, and Meg asking about The Dead Men.

"You're not seriously doing... something... are you?" Baker slurred, glazed eyes directed back at Meg.

"I... thought it'd be cool."

"It will be cool!" Kay shouted. Meg was starting to feel slightly embarrassed of her in this company.

Baker drolly gave a look at Kay, then back at Meg and snorted a chuckle, waving his finger at her. He began to say something but instead starting laughing, the boob girl joining in. Meg was starting to feel more and more uncomfortable, paranoid at being the little girl she really was within this crowd.

"Try the cemetery?" Baker finally offered, rolling from one position to another. "Dead Men usually are there!"

"No shit!" Boob girl offered, and the two burst into laughter again.

Meg gave her thanks and dragged Kay away with her at speed. She didn't like this place at night. It was tainted, from the cool comic decoration to Baker and his ways. It made her shake with negative emotion, while Kay was too oblivious to what was surely mocking tones at their expense.

"Hey Meg!" Baker shouted before they left.

She looked back and saw Baker leaning drunkenly off the table he was at, staring at her.

"You're a cute kid, try not to get nicked!"

She felt quite flustered at this sudden compliment, and instead of offering some cool retort she just turned around and kept walking, her face turning a bright shade of crimson. However her fluttering heart was shaken again when someone shouted at them after they were through the door.

"They're coming to get you Barbara!" They slurred, to a chorus of insane laughter.

The local cemetery was a short walk from the high street, hidden in the midst of several cheap, cookie-cutter residential roads. You couldn't miss it though, as it stood out like a sore thumb in comparison to the flat complexes and garden/drive semi's that lined it. It seemed to thrive on the gothic ideal, the gate that let you in large and imposing and flanked by statues of birds weathered by time. For Meg and Kay, it wasn't so much intimidating as creepy as Hell.

By now, the sun had fully set and the only light came from the moon in the sky and Kay's mobile. She had taken to live-tweeting their adventures, occasionally dictating them to Meg as she typed.

"I've just tweeted 'entering the graveyard. It's spooky as anything!'"

Meg didn't bother answering. After all, how could you answer such inane observations? Instead she was recording, getting her pick up's as best she could in the gloom. Kay was right when she said the place was spooky. Meg thought about how it was inbuilt in people's minds that in the moonlight graves are chilling sights. The stone epitaphs silhouetted in the grey and cast long shadows against a darker floor.

The graves stretched back for a mile or two, neatly lined up and varying in size and shape. Some were simple stones, with the basic details on them regarding the deceased, while some had elaborate designs depicting angels, crosses or other pseudo-spiritual motifs. In the day they would look fairly innocuous, but in the night they were striking, almost alive. Monuments to a life once lived, defying you not to take in their majesty.

The two girls decided to settle up on a bench halfway down the central walk-way. It was getting colder, the weather added to the chill the two were experiencing. Kay adjusted her coat as Meg continued to film, taking in as much as she could.

"So when do you think they'll get here?" She whispered.

"No idea."

"So... we just wait?"

Meg looked at her friend. "This was your idea, remember?"

Kay just pulled a face and went back to her phone, tweeting 'Who knew the dead were so boring? LOLZ!'

An hour passed, and in that time all Meg had on her camera were a few interesting gravestones and the dead flowers that littered them. Hardly Oscar-winning stuff. By now Kay's enthusiasm had dissipated and she had begun a constant routine of attention-grabbing huffs and foot-stomping. For the most part Meg ignored her, but occasionally she'd bite and remind Kay of her "hero" statement earlier.

"I don't think they'll turn up."

Meg thought for a moment and felt inclined to agree.

"It's still early though."

"Early? It's 10! My Mum will be shitting if she knew I was out!"

"Where are you then?"

"Round yours."

Meg shot Kay a look. "I'm round yours!"

Both girls looked at each other worried, before something caught their ear.

Across the graveyard two men were lurking, armed with heavy bags. The Dead Men. Meg instantly threw up her camera and started recording, Kay hiding behind her.

"There they are!"

"Shh!"

"How exciting..."

The two of them creeped between the gravestones, careful not to be seen by the two men as they stopped and started sifting through their bags. Meg zoomed in on them and watched as they produced strange equipment from them. First it was things that were obvious, like torches that they flashed on and off to test, but then there were things like those nooses people use to control dogs and something that caught the glare of the moon and shined toward the girls.

They ducked behind a large gravestone, which had an angel looking down upon them. Kay was giggling with exhilaration while Meg tried to keep her hand steady and record the Dead Men. She watched as they looked around the cemetery, making notes and pointing to various plots. The older one, Winston van Huhn, seemed to be directing while Craig Vale jotted things down. *Master and apprentice*, Meg assumed.

As the two girls watched, neither heard something rustle behind them. Their intensity at stalking The Dead Men had enraptured them so much that the sound of earth moving from the grave across the path was lost in the wind whistling past.

"What do you think they're doing?"

"I've no idea Kay!"

"Do you think they're deciding which body to nick?"

"How should I know?"

"Well maybe..."

Before Kay could finish she felt a presence behind her. Quickly, she turned round and let out an ear-piercing scream reserved only for the lowest grade horror movies. Just as swift and with camera in hand, Meg turned round and in her viewfinder, caught the colourless, mouldy skin of a zombie in her sights. While Kay managed to sprint toward the cemetery's entrance, Meg just dropped her camera and let it carry on recording at her feet, documenting the zombies feet shamble over to hers. She was frozen into place with terror, just watching as this undead horror groaned and reached toward her. All she thought of was how ironic this was. Her, a star in her own horror movie, about to die at the hands of the creature she idolized.

As it got closer, Meg felt all the blood leave her body and everything go very dark as she hit the ground with a THUD.

As Meg's eyes twitched open she was immediately blinded by a bright light. For a moment, she thought she was in Heaven, her spirit making it's way to Nirvana while her physical body was no doubt being slowly digested by some horrible flesh-eater.

The truth soon dawned though, and was much more mundane. Well, relatively speaking. Kneeling before her, as she rested on the grave she had been hiding behind, was Winston van Huhn.

"Are you OK?"

"Course she's bloody OK!" Meg heard someone shout.

"Well, we have to check these things." van Huhn continued, shining his torch on Meg and studying her head. He reached out and carefully touched the top of her head.

"Ouch!" She uttered, a nasty cut had formed on her forehead where she had fainted.

"Ah I think you'll survive."

Van Huhn smiled warmly at her and stood up. He was dressed in the overalls they had seen him in the other day with his long hair tied tightly back. Behind him, Kay stood shivering and ashamed while Vale stared at them both and looked ready to bollock them.

"Come on, get up." van Huhn said, offering a hand.

Meg took it and pulled herself up. She steadied herself a bit before Kay rushed over and hugged her, offering a litany of apologies. She had *panicked... shat herself... lost her nerve...* all perfectly acceptable excuses given the situation. Meg was just standing there dumbfounded, watching as van Huhn went over to Vale and began to talk. Vale was more animated and angry, gesturing towards the girls viciously with a face contorted with bile. However, van Huhn was doing his best to placate his protege, and eventually Vale calmed down and the two approached the girls.

"So, care to tell us what you're doing out here at this time of night?"

Neither girl answered, instead resorting to the stereotype of lowering their heads and kicking their heels.

"Hey, he asked you a question!"

"We... we were just..."

"We thought we'd make a film about you..." Meg meekly offered.

This response took both men by surprise, with Vale's lip turning further up his face with confusion. His partner, however, looked quite intrigued.

"Why?"

"Because we thought you were grave robbers and that it'd be cool?"

Once again, Meg's words caused a reaction in The Dead Men, as they both stood stunned before bursting into laughter, looking at each other knowingly.

Van Huhn shook his head and looked back at Meg. "You think we steal bodies?"

"That's what Baker said down the pub!" Kay blurted.

"Bloody knobhead..." Vale said, shaking his head. "What does he know? Spends most of his time getting tanked and staring at Fi's tits!"

Meg bristled at this, but instead just looked at van Huhn. "We're sorry, we'll leave you alone from now, I promise."

Van Huhn stroked his beard as only a man of his age could, and looked back at Vale. The younger's smile faded away as he looked at his colleague.

"No. No, just... no Win!"

"Could be fun."

"We'd get bollocked!"

Van Huhn shrugged. "I think it's time people should know."

Vale just waved his hand and dismissed him, turning back and collecting his stuff. Van Huhn turned back to the girls, primarily Meg, and smiled.

"Why don't you meet us in the Arms tomorrow, say about 2ish, and we'll discuss your film."

Meg nodded and found herself gripping onto Kay, who was doing the same in kind. Van Huhn took a deep breath, looked around the graveyard and then back at the girls.

"For tonight though, we need to work. So I think you should..."

Van Huhn didn't finish, instead gesturing to the entrance. The girls didn't need telling twice, almost jogging back to where they entered.

As they left the cemetery, Meg looked round to see van Huhn wave at her, and Vale pull up something corpse-like with the noose they had been carrying.

Kay had ended up staying the night round Meg's, giving some level of credence to their conflicting stories in the end. Surprisingly, she had been rather silent about the whole affair and the two girls had just got on with things. They slept, had breakfast and Kay made small talk with Meg's parents before they left the house, camera in hand, to once again meet with The Dead Men.

As they walked down the hill to the high street, Kay grabbed onto Meg's arm and let it all out.

"What the Fuck happened last night!?"

Meg was slightly taken aback by the suddenness of Kay's question, but managed to compose herself.

"I don't know. But hopefully we're gonna find out."

"Was it some sort of prank? It had to be a prank..."

"Well I don't know do I? I passed out..."

"It had to be a prank..." Kay continued.

"Well you were still conscious, what did you see?"

"I don't know. I hid behind a grave until those two weirdo's came along."

Meg rolled her eyes and kept walking. It was nearly 2 and they were close to the Arms. Despite what had happened last night, she was even more intrigued by the two men known locally as The Dead Men. Whatever they were doing, it wasn't grave-robbing. It was something far more cool, but Meg needed to hear them say the words before assuming anything.

As they entered the pub, Kay still nervously mumbling about being "tricked", Meg saw the two men sat casually in the garden. Van Huhn offered a friendly wave, and the girls made their way over and sat down, ready to hear them out.

While Kay just plastered on her fake smile, Meg engaged in some small talk with van Huhn, before eventually asking the thing that was bothering her most of all.

"Are you guys zombie hunters?"

It sounded ridiculous once she had put it out there, and in fact both men had just responded with large grins and raised eyebrows. Van Huhn took a sip of his ale and shook his head before thinking this over.

"I wouldn't quite put it that way." he answered.

"Yeah it ain't no Buffy type shenanigans." Vale continued, puffing on his pipe.

"But, that was a..."

"Zombie? Again, you could say that."

"Well was it or wasn't it?"

"I think I need a drink for this." Kay interrupted, and made her excuses to depart, leaving Meg alone with them. She glared at them for an answer.

"By definition, yeah I suppose it was." Vale eventually answered. "But prob not what you're thinking of."

"You're probably thinking all 'Brains!' and George Romero films, right?"

"No." Meg said. She was.

"Well, it's not quite like that. Myself and Craig work as wranglers, making sure the dead, well..."

"Stay dead."

The more the two men described their job, the more Meg became fascinated. The Dead Men were hired by the council, under the label of 'Pest Control', and that zombies were very, very real. And not Voodoo real but rise-out-the-grave real. What Meg had seen last night was, indeed, a member of the undead, and it both frightened and excited her.

"So why did it attack me?" She asked.

"Did it?" Vale retorted with more than a hint of sarcasm.

"It was reaching at you, but it wasn't going to attack you."

"We get half a dozen Reachers a week. They see a person and immediately they're like 'Hey! Who are you? Give us a hug!'"

Both men burst into laughter, sipping away at their drinks and recounting tales of Reachers they had encountered with each other. As Meg listened she saw the two had a camaraderie you saw in buddy movies, the young, intense rookie teamed with the wiser veteran. Her finger was itching to bring up the camera and catch it all on film, for the record.

She felt this was a good as any to bring the subject up.

"So my film..."

"Oh yes."

"Well, first it was gonna be an expose..."

"What of us robbing graves? Pfft, I wish..." Vale scoffed.

"It would most likely be more lucrative." van Huhn continued.

"Well, yes, but what you do sounds *way* more interesting!"

The two men looked at each other, then van Huh addressed Meg again.

"Technically what we do is top secret, but there's no actual rules on speaking to people. What were you planning to do with this film?"

"Um, put it on Youtube?"

Van Huhn nodded and then turned back to Vale, who simply shrugged and finished up his drink.

"OK, well how about you join us on a... 'hunt', tonight?"

Meg lit up with fervour. She started nodding far too much and mentally shouted at herself to stop, doing it so suddenly that no doubt it looked weird.

"That way we can explain the ins and outs of what we do, give you some live examples."

Meg was now smiling far too much now, and desperately tried to put on a more professional appearance. She was turning all fan-boy at this talk of zombies and hunting, and was feeling quite giddy at the concept of following the men around as they tackled the undead.

As he put his coat on, Vale nodded across the garden. "You can even invite your friend along, if she's not busy."

He grinned like a cheshire cat and as Meg looked over she saw why. Kay had got distracted and was deep in conversation with Baker, flirtatious conversation. She felt her blood boil as she became more and more jealous with every hair flick and over-the-top laugh Kay did. As The Dead Men walked away, Meg stood there and watched the two talk, with Kay only eventually turning round to acknowledge her friend. Before she could speak, Meg just picked up her bag and stormed past her, too upset to speak. Her pace was so fast she overtook van Huhn and Vale and felt her ears burn as she zipped into the high street and toward home. She wasn't even aware that she was crying.

Various text alerts flashed on her phone as Meg prepared for her night with The Dead Men. Since running from the pub, it had been a constant barrage of beeps and musical ringtones from Kay trying to contact her. But Meg was in no mood to talk, she was focussing on her evening seeing zombies in real life and getting to make her new film. It was a better film than the one she had been doing, and plus she didn't have Kay doing her lame impression to bring down the whole thing. This would be real, and therefore have more value.

She had managed to convince her parents that this was part of a college project, something she had arranged through her Video Production class and was all above board. Mentioning that The Dead Men were council workers further put their minds at ease, but her Mum had offered the usual over-protective mantra. As well as a packed lunch.

Armed with her equipment, Meg made her way back to the cemetery she had run from the night before. It was already full dark when she arrived, and the cold was easing in. She adjusted her jacket tightly and waited by the gates.

She didn't need to wait long. After 5 minutes a white van pulled up to the curb with a council logo adorning it. Inside sat van Huhn and Vale, already in their uniforms and all business. After getting out, Vale produced a sign he put on the windshield and van Huhn made his way over to Meg.

"So, ready?"

Meg just nodded, smiling giddily. Her heart was beating fast as the excitement of what was about to happen slowly dawned on her. She was going to see a real life zombie be captured, or killed, or something, by real life zombie hunters. It was crazy, but it was so cool.

Van Huhn grabbed a large bag from the back of the van and motioned for Meg to follow. Vale meandered behind them collecting another holdall and closing the gates of the cemetery, putting up another sign.

"A little precaution after your adventures the other night." van Huhn explained.

He led her up to the far end of the cemetery, where a small shed stood. With a set of keys van Huhn opened it up and turned on a light, revealing a place filled with minimal amenities. They both put their bags down while Meg watched Vale prepare a cup of tea.

"Never work on an empty stomach, first rule of employment."

Vale offered, but Meg turned down a cup of tea, instead producing a bottle of juice from her bag. She stood there as the two men sipped tea and talked about various inane subjects such as football, music and other stuff that Meg had heard men talk about all the time. After a while, van Huhn turned to her and nodded at her bag.

"You might want to start filming soon."

Meg nervously nodded in agreement and fumbled out her camera. While she did, the two men began sifting through their large bags, producing their equipment.

"Zombies, or Moaners as we like to call them, aren't the nasty little shits the films make them out to be." Vale explained, armed with one of the nooses Meg had seen the night before. "They're more of a pest, like rats or roaches or something. But obviously you can't poison or blow them up or anything like that."

"People tend to get a little... irritable if their loved ones are decimated in a controlled explosion." van Huhn added.

"So our job is to get rid of them by putting them back where they belong. In the ground."

Meg kept the camera focussed on the two men as they pulled items out of bags. As well as the noose-sticks, there were the torches and, which surprised Meg, large handheld mirrors.

"What are they for?" She asked.

Van Huhn looked at the mirror and smiled. "You'll see soon enough. Come on, let's get to work."

The Dead Men made their way back into the graveyard with Meg filming behind them. She recorded as they surveyed the land, commenting on recent ground movement and any potential Moaner locations.

"Most Moaners tend to be fresh, so you look for new arrivals." Vale explained.

"It's the mentality, they don't like to give up being alive so easily you see."

Meg just nodded along in silence, it was all quite something to take in. The Dead Men were so casual in their approach, looking over the graves with mental precision and highlighting what was new and what looked disturbed. She followed as they stepped between the graves, looking over the dirt and taking it all in.

"Usually the council will provide us with a list of recent deaths, hence why we've been here the last couple of nights." van Huhn stated.

"Newbies can usually take up to a week to surface, depending on how strong they are and how crap the ground is."

As Meg tracked across the cemetery, something caught her eye in the viewfinder. Whatever it was, it was shuffling uncomfortably around before standing up straight.

"Is that.... is that one?" she asked, noticing how quiet she was.

The Dead Men looked over and nodded, with van Huhn offering Meg a friendly pat on the back. They picked up their nooses and torches and made their way over to the 'Moaner'.

Once they were close enough Meg zoomed in to get a good look at the undead creature. It was a women, quite young and beautiful and decked out in a wonderful white dressed stained with dirt. However, one side of her temple was crushed in and marked with blood from where she had been hit. While Meg recorded the zombie as it stood there, jaw loose and mild groans emanating from it's throat, Vale and van Huhn were consulting a piece of paper.

"Kirsty Puller, died from severe head trauma."

"Looks like they did a shit job fixing her up."

The undead Puller didn't really notice the three of them at first, instead marvelling in dumb awe at the starry night above her. She gave the occasional groan as her face twitched and vaguely emoted, but mostly she just stood there, star-gazing.

Vale grabbed the noose while van Huhn picked up a torch and mirror. He made his way in front of Puller while Vale checked the ground from where she had risen from. It had collapsed in a bit, but still had enough of a hole.

Meg recorded intently as the two men went to work. She watched through the viewfinder as van Huhn stood in front and began flashing the torch on and off in Puller's face. Eventually, her head slumped forward and she stared in a stupor at van Huhn. She began to raise her arms and lurch toward him, but he quickly shone the torch in her face and produced the mirror. It lit up her pale and dried features horribly in the reflection, and the zombie Puller's face went from intrigue to horror as she stared at herself.

From behind, Vale threaded the noose round her neck and clicked it tight. With a light but quick tug, he put Puller to the floor next to the grave she had risen from. He held her down while she lurched a little bit.

"The thing you gotta do with Moaners is, well, confuse them. And nothing confuses them more than seeing themselves in their dead state. You see their brains are... well they're all messed up. So they see themselves like that and..."

With his free hand Vale put two fingers to his head like a gun and made a SPLAT noise. From beside them, van Huhn had arrived with a shovel.

"You have a beautiful way with words." van Huhn said.

"Why thank you, I feel I am a verbose individual."

The two men laughed as van Huhn began digging at the disturbed earth and Vale rolled Puller's now limp body back in. Within a few minutes the grave was settled again and the undead back where it belonged, under the ground.

Meg stood there filming. The Dead Men just celebrated another job well done and gathered up their belongings. At one stage, Vale looked deep into the camera and winked.

"Welcome to the wonderful world of pest control." He said with a smile.

They both started making their way back to the shed while Meg got one final shot of Puller's grave. She held it there for a few minutes, getting details of the epitaph, before shutting the viewfinder and with that, turning off the camera.

All she could think was: *that was it?*

She picked up the pace and joined The Dead Men back at their shed, where Vale was marking off on a sheet while van Huhn munched on a sandwich. She looked at them both and waited, before grabbing van Huhn's attention.

"So what now?"

Van Huhn didn't answer at first, instead finishing his mouthful. Vale carried on with his paperwork.

"I mean, is it dead? As in dead dead?"

"Well *she* was already dead."

"Yes, but, do you have to re-enforce the grave or anything in case it, she, comes back?"

Vale laughed to himself as he listened while van Huhn just ate another bit of his sandwich.

"Once you show them that they are dead, they tend to stay dead. It's the main focus of wrangling."

Meg thought about this for a moment before shaking her head. "I don't understand."

"The undead are, like Craig said, pests." van Huhn explained. "What we do is show them they are dead and then put them back to rest. That's it."

"Light 'em, noose 'em, bury 'em." Vale clarified.

"So... no hunting?"

"No hunting."

Meg couldn't help but feel a little disappointed.

They stayed at the cemetery for another hour, waiting in case any other Moaner's rose up, before The Dead Men gave Meg a lift home on their way to their next location. It was late anyway, and van Huhn warned Meg that she didn't want to get into the world of night work.

"Fucks up your body clock like a bitch." Vale stated more bluntly.

Despite it not being the thrill a minute adventure she was expecting, Meg still wanted to follow these guys in their work, and agreed to meet them later on tomorrow for more interviews. As she watched them drive off, she couldn't help but wonder if there was anything more that they were protecting from her.

Either way, Meg made her way indoors, said hello to her parents, and entered her room, where she saw her phone flashing away on the bed, rejected. She picked it up and saw that most were notifications of missed calls and texts from Kay, confused as to why she had stormed off before. Too tired to bother going into the drama it would entail, Meg just cleared them all and turned the phone off, collapsing into bed and sighing.

The following day bought another barrage of messages from Kay for Meg to ignore. It was tricky, as she had time to kill before setting off to meet with van Huhn at the address he had given her. Due to their night work, she had agreed to meet with him at 6 and Vale an hour later, before heading off with both men for another night of "zombie-wrangling".

While she was certainly persistent with her texts, Meg was more hacked off at the lack of calls from Kay. Hell, even coming round in person would be a start, so there would be less of this back and forth over the phone. But no, every hour or so another text would land asking the same thing:

AV I DUN SUMFIN? :(

It wasn't just the complete lack of realization at what she'd done, or even the lack of direct contact, it was also the irritating use of TXT speak and general common attitude that Kay had adopted in recent times. Meg didn't want to say it, but she was starting to feel a little bit better than Kay in terms of who she was. Kay was interested in boys and drinking, while Meg was more focussed on doing something. She didn't know why they were friends anymore.

The time came around though and Meg started making her way to van Huhn's address. He wasn't based too far away from her parents, a couple of miles up the nice area of town. When she got to the number, she saw it was a nice terraced house with a front garden and drive, something you'd expect of a family man. In fact, after she knocked the front door, she was greeted by a large-set woman with a homely look about her.

"You must be Meg? I'm Jean, Winston's wife."

Jean motioned for Meg to enter, allowing her to take in the full domesticity of Winston van Huhn's home life. The house was your typical affair, with a large living room and kitchen/dining room that led to a sizable garden decorated with various plants, a BBQ and a small allotment down the end.

Meg fiddled with her camera and asked Jean if she could record. "Go ahead love! Just try not to get me on camera."

"Oh, I was hoping to ask a few questions..."

"OK, well I don't mind that just try not to show me, I look a mess!" Jean giggled, adjusting her curly hair.

Meg did some pans of van Huhn's house while trading a few casual questions and answers with Jean about their life. They had been friends for a few years and been married for 2, with Jean being van Huhn's second wife. Apparently van Huhn's first wife wasn't a fan of his night work and absconded, but that was all that was said on that matter. Regarding her reaction to his work, Jean didn't really take an interest.

"After all, I married the man, not his job!" She clarified with a giggle.

After a few minutes van Huhn arrived, looking casual in denim jeans and a T-shirt adorned by some obscure rock band from a bygone era. Meg filmed his entrance out of habit, earning a curious look from her subject.

"Do excuse me, I've just been blowing up communists on the Eastern Front."

Meg looked at Jean confused, who just chuckled again.

"Him and his war games. I swear, he's obsessed."

He smiled and moved over to give an affectionate peck to his other half. After a bit of coupley banter, Jean left the two of them be to film the interview at the dining table. While van Huhn made himself comfortable, Meg messed around with setting up the tripod that she had rarely used. She was sure eventually she would be an expert at adjusting it's various levers and screws, but at the moment she watched in frustration as the camera mounted on top kept falling forward. Eventually, after many experimental tugs and twists, it stayed firm with van Huhn fully in shot.

Meg had prepared some generic questions to ask them both, ideally hoping that their answers would open up more interesting subjects. She started by asking van Huhn how he got into this work. His response was rather bland.

"I answered an advert in the paper." He shrugged.

Meg decided to go straight for the meat of the interview; the zombies. She wanted to know what it was like tackling them and if he ever got afraid. After all, it was a unique experience.

"I think first of all it was quite shocking." van Huhn confessed, "But my senior at the time was very precise and informative. He quickly dispelled any myths there was surrounding them."

"You didn't think they'd be flesh eating monsters?"

Van Huhn shook his head. "Not at all. I mean, you see a lot of things on film but once you see them in real life, so to speak, you see how docile and harmless they are."

Meg then took a different approach, asking more detailed questions regarding the violence and horror of it all. Alas, van Huhn's response were still quite average. There was no real gory content, most bodies being well prepared by morticians. As for any horror, the zombies were simply mindless creatures who were adjusting to another state of being. Getting to grips with being dead.

"So you've never been attacked?" Meg asked.

"Nope. They just don't do that sort of thing."

"But what about when they reach for you? What happens when they grab you?"

"Oh, well, they grab you, not viciously but rather softly, look at you and try to figure out what you are. As my colleague says, they're a little 'messed up'."

Aha, van Huhn's colleague Craig Vale. If Meg couldn't get a horror theme to this film, she'd be best getting a human element. After all, the two seemed very different; van Huhn the wise old sage while Vale was the boisterous young buck following in his footsteps. Van Huhn laughed at the analogy.

"Well yes, Craig is a rambunctious fellow, but he's taken very well to the job."

"You don't seem like you'd get along?" Meg asked, hoping for some sort of story.

134

"Maybe, but then you and your friend are quite different aren't you?"

Meg felt herself retract a little. She had been trying not to think about Kay. After all, out of sight, out of mind. However van Huhn was right.

"The thing is, while we're very different people, we just seem to gel." van Huhn continued. "Craig is feisty, but he's a good person and a good friend. Just because we're not exactly similar, doesn't mean we can't work together."

These words hit Meg hard, and she couldn't get her old friend out of her head now.

"After all, opposites attract." van Huhn concluded.

Craig Vale's place was much different to van Huhn's domestic lodgings. First of all, it was part of a flat complex, positioned on the ground floor and lacking any sort of garden or outside space. Inside it was deceptively larger, but still nothing compared to the home of his fellow zombie-wrangler.

Vale had greeted Meg at the door and led her through the short hallway which connected all the rooms. She followed him to the Living Room, where a scruffy looking man lay on the sofa playing video games surrounded by very minimalist décor.

"Dude, piss off, I've got an interview."

"Ah 5 minutes, I'm nearly finished!" the scruff argued in a thick Welsh brogue.

Vale wasn't listening though, and quickly shooed his friend from the room, offering promises of pints as some sort of compensation. It worked, and soon Meg found herself alone with the young Dead Man. He was dressed incredibly casually, in some sort of velour jogging bottoms and a black hoodie covering his long hair. As Meg set up her camera, he slouched back into the sofa and picked at his ear.

"So what sort of things you gonna be asking?"

"Um, well just how doing your job affects your life, what it's like, that sort of thing."

"Well don't think you're gonna get your mind blown." Vale remarked.

He was right. His path to the job was similar to van Huhn's. An advert in the local job centre, a flexibility to working nights and finally an apathy towards the subject of the undead.

"First time I saw a Moaner sure, I nearly pissed himself." He confessed. "But once you realize how gormless they are, it takes the sting off a little."

Vale explained he had worked in the job for 2 years, teaming with van Huhn all the way. He spoke highly of his co-worker, touting his experience and jocular manner.

"When you do a job like this an entertainment factor is highly appreciated. Most of the time you're hanging around in graveyards twiddling your thumbs. You'd join the bastards if you were with some boring cunt."

Vale's manner was as bombastic as it was on the job, and, if Meg was honest, she felt a tad uncomfortable in the man's presence. But listening to him speak there was a sense that there was something more to him. That maybe van Huhn's manner was rubbing off on him somewhat.

"Thing is, in this job you get to see a side of life that you rarely *do* see. Death."

"What do you mean?" Meg asked, curious as to where Vale was going with this.

"Well, when you see the Moaners and Reachers stumbling around, looking quite lost, you kinda think to yourself don't you?"

Meg urged him to continue.

"What I mean is, they look so... regretful. Maybe that's why they come back, because they feel like they haven't finished something. That they've left something unfulfilled. Because I mean they don't always come back. Some stay dead, it's just the odd one that pops it's head back up that we have to plough down again."

"Does it make you sad to see them like that?"

Vale scoffed. "Nah. Not sad. Just... I dunno. Pity really. I mean, if you take that thought then they must feel like shit. I mean who's to say in your last moments, your last thoughts, don't stay with you. Thoughts of regret, of loves you didn't confess, opportunities you didn't take, hatchets you didn't bury."

Once again, Meg's mind went to Kay. She started to feel a bit guilty.

"At the end of the day, I think what the dead teach ya, is that you only live once. After that, it's nothing. Not really. I mean I don't believe in God or any of that bollocks, so when they pop back up again, it's like they want a second chance. But they won't get it. Not anymore."

Meg was silent after Vale said this. She had been a fool getting all jealous with Kay, her oldest friend, over some random guy in the pub who was old enough to be her... well. Not her father but definitely an older, older brother.

"I will say this, the money is a nice fucking bonus!" Vale remarked, letting out a sharp laugh to punctuate it.

Meg gathered her thoughts and thanked Vale, packing up her equipment and deciding to do whatever it took to find Kay again and make up. Before she left, Vale called out to her.

"Don't forget, we're on again tonight. You might see something interesting. Has to happen eventually!"

Making her way home, the first thing Meg did was finally reply to Kay's texts. She didn't want to completely sound like she was being a wuss and backing down, after all Kay did start flirting with someone she kind of liked. Instead, she sent a generic text asking how she was. What she got in reply was a phone call.

"Oh my God I'm so sorry I didn't mean to upset you because I know you'd be upset because I was talking to Baker and you so obviously fancy him and I didn't think and I'm sorry!" Kay said, without taking a breath.

Meg smiled as she listened. "It's cool, sorry I was being a bit of a dick."

"You weren't a dick! I was a dick! I'm so, so sorry! Besties still?"

Meg answered the best way she knew how in these situations.

"Pub?"

At The Patterson Arms the two girls celebrated their reconciliation with a toast of ciders, drinking them with good cheer and mutual banter. At one stage Baker did appear, giving his usual greetings to them both and Meg found herself looking at him a different way. Yes he was cool, but he was just a guy who went to the pub, and not someone worth fighting over or losing a friend. She greeted him back, had a little bit of small talk before turning back to Kay. When it came to boys, Meg was happy to wait it out.

After all, she had a film to make.

"So what was it like? Was it all gross and scary?" Kay asked.

"Not really, it was quite boring actually."

"Boring?"

"Yeah. They just kinda shone a torch in one's face and held a mirror at it."

Kay just looked at Meg with the weirdest expression she had ever seen. It was a combination of confusion and suspicious.

"They showed them their reflection?"

"Yeah."

"Why?"

"To show them they were dead."

Kay just looked at her for a second.

"That's the dumbest thing I ever heard."

And with that, they both burst into a fit of giggles.

"I'm joining them again tonight if you fancy tagging along?"

"Yeah! As long as I won't get attacked like last time..."

"Um, I got attacked. Remember?"

"Yeah well..."

"Anyway, apparently they just... look at you."

"Meg, the more you tell me about this, the more it sounds completely weird. As in, shit weird."

Meg shrugged and finished her drink. "Come along tonight and see for yourself."

When they arrived at the cemetery The Dead Men were already engaged in a hive of activity. While Vale looked over some paperwork, van Huhn was on the phone with someone. As the two girls stumbled along, a little worse for wear, Vale gave them a look.

"Didn't think you were turning up!"

"Would you have missed me?" Meg slurred, before giggling along with Kay.

Vale's eyes widened as he saw the girls were drunk and looked over to van Huhn. He was listening on the phone but shot the girls a look to show he wasn't impressed.

"So what's going down Mr Vale?" Meg asked with her camera in hand. Beside her, Kay was trying to prop herself up.

"Well, I promised you excitement and here it is. We got a Lurker."

With that the two of them suddenly sobered up a little.

"What's a Lurker?" Kay asked.

"It's a Moaner who's fucked off."

It was Kay's turn to widen her eyes this time. "Where?"

Vale ignored her and continued making notes as van Huhn finished up on the phone.

"Apparently it's heading down Rutland. If we head off now we should intercept it." He said, before turning to the girls. "You two can get in the back if you want."

Vale casually opened the doors and showed the girls in. There wasn't much room, and nowhere to really sit and strap in. In the doorway, The Dead Men looked at them.

"Get comfy, it's a bumpy ride." Vale said, smiling before shutting the door.

The only light came from a small window to the front seats, where van Huhn and Vale eventually appeared. For a moment both girls were scared, of both the idea of a Lurker and being in the back of a windowless van.

"What if this has been all a ruse?" Kay whispered.

"Don't be stupid!" Meg hissed, but the thought did make her paranoid.

The van started up and sure enough, the ride was an uncomfortable one. The girls clung onto each other to steady themselves as The Dead Men threw the van round corners and over hills. Pushing onto the side to get her footing, Meg shouted through the window, passing the camera to Kay.

"What's a Lurker?"

"I've already told you!" Vale shouted back.

"Yeah, but, is it bad?"

"It's annoying."

"Will it, like, do anything?"

"Maybe..."

"Oh stop frightening them Craig!" van Huhn shouted, eyes fixed on the road.

Vale turned to the girls and smiled. "You ever see those people lurching around at night, like they're pissed. Kinda like you."

Both girls nodded.

"Well sometimes they're Lurkers, Moaners that have flown the nest and heading home."

"Most of the time people ignore them, but you get the odd person who gets worried and calls the Police, who then call us."

"Like now?" Meg asked.

"Like now."

"And then you get the stupid bastards who try and mug them." Vale continued. "That's a hilarity."

"Why?"

"Because they're threatening with a knife and shit, and this Moaner is looking at them all glassy eyed. Then, next thing the mugger knows this Moaner becomes a Reacher and they grow some balls and stab it and it falls on them!"

Before he could finish Vale started laughing hysterically, van Huhn joining in. Both girls just looked at each other, oblivious to the in-joke as Vale settled back in his seat.

"They never say anything about it, mostly because they get caught or freaked out. It's just bloody funny when you find them with piss-stained pants and a Moaner gone dead again on top... ooh there it is!"

Both girls strained to look out the tiny window, but Meg managed to squeeze the camera through. Sure enough, walking up the pavement was a Moaner, or Lurker as Vale was calling it. The Dead Men exchanged tactics, before van Huhn pulled up to the curb. Quick as a flash, Vale jumped out and Meg listened as he ran around the van and opened the door.

"I apologise in advance." He said, grabbing a noose.

"What does he mean by that?" Kay asked, as Meg kept recording.

Vale disappeared and they listened as van Huhn provided commentary, giving Vale instructions. After a few moments, van Huhn began congratulating Vale and started the car up again.

Meg looked over to the window to talk, but was distracted by Kay screaming. She looked over and saw Vale with the Lurker at the end of the pole. He shoved it in the back with the girls, who scurried up the back wall of the van. Vale threw in the noose, looked at the girls with a shrug, and then shut them in with a zombie.

Meg heard Kay begin to cry, but with shaking hands held up her camera to film the zombie. As the van began to pull away, she watched as it just lay there completely oblivious to what was going, before the motion of the van rolled it over. It managed to lurch up into a sitting position and turned to look straight down Meg's viewfinder. Kay gibbered some nonsensical ramblings as The Dead Men casually nattered in the front seat. Meg kept filming, and felt herself looking in the eyes of the so-called Moaner as it looked down the lens. It seemed sad, almost lost, much like Vale had said. It almost broke Meg's heart to see what used to be a human being look so devoid of life, but be so unaware of it's state. In that moment she realized the true horror of a zombie wasn't the flesh-eating or virus-spreading or anything like that, it was the loss of humanity, losing what made you, you and becoming just a shell.

Eventually, the Moaner lay back down and stayed there while The Dead Men drove them back to the cemetery where it belonged.

Meg didn't sleep that night. Not out of fear of being shut in a van with a zombie, although that was Kay's excuse, but more of what she had seen within it. It made her think about what The Dead Men had said about life, about those who you share your life with and making sure you take advantage of this time and not regretting a thing. By staring death in the face, so to speak, she saw the emptiness it left you with. She didn't want that feeling.

The next afternoon, when both girls finally rose, Meg had a plan.

"I need to finish this film." She told Kay. "It needs to be seen."

"OK..."

"It's going on tonight. I'm editing it tonight."

And she did. She grabbed all her SD cards full of footage and put it all on her computer. Kay was tasked with supplies, and returned with a few energy drinks and nibbles, as well as moral support.

"So what do you think people will think of this?"

"I don't know. I don't care." Meg curtly replied, her focus intense on the screen.

She finally had her story. The Dead Men weren't grave-robbers or zombie-hunters, they were normal people like them who did an abnormal job. But in essence, their job was one of great merit. They took those who had lost their way after death, who were filled with sadness and an inability to let go, and they helped them gain peace. It wasn't Meg and Kay who were the heroes in making this film, it was Winston van Huhn and Craig Vale. They were the ones who were doing a noble job that no-one spoke of, for fear of freaking out the populace. They needed to be recognised in Meg's eyes, the *deserved* to be recognised, and she'd bring them that recognition.

She jotted out a narration and sent Kay away to read it into a Dictaphone. She had done drama, and was capable of being a good orator outside of her usual common tongue. When she returned, Meg was almost finished, doing the final tweaks and edits. After uploading the narration and adjusting that to fit the footage she had plotted out, Meg began creating the film: The Dead Men.

After her computer alerted it was done, Kay turned to her.

"So what now?"

"Now we show everyone." Meg replied, pride in her voice.

She uploaded the film to Youtube, and spread the word via social networks. Over the next 2 hours the views poured in, people lured in with the promise of zombies and then being hit with a very human story instead. Meg felt quite good about herself as she saw the numbers add up, Kay spreading the word via text as well.

She had done it, she had made a film.

"I think we should celebrate don't you?"

The two girls acquired a bottle of cider and toasted to the films success. When they left it, the numbers had entered triple digits and looked unlikely to stop climbing. With each drop, the two friends also bonded once more, giggling over silly jokes and tales of boys and mutual friends and other silly stuff that they had done in their youth.

As Meg finished her second glass, she turned to the computer.

"Let's see if we're in the millions!" She announced with glee.

However there was a problem. When she clicked the link she was greeted with a message saying the film no longer existed. After a few more clicks, she went into her account to see an email saying that the video had been reported and taken down.

"Who'd do that?" Kay screamed, cursing the mystery persons name.

Meg didn't know, and endeavoured to find out. She went through links and messages and forums to try and gather some information, and eventually got it in the form of the account that had taken umbrage at her work.

It was registered to the Council.

"Bastards!" Kay exclaimed.

"Bugger them, I'll have words in the morning." Meg slurred, before putting her glass down and falling into bed.

The next day, both Meg and Kay, as well as their hangovers, made their way to the council offices. The building was a brown, modest place, hidden away by trees and a long entrance which kept it hidden from angry passer-bys.

Once they entered, Meg stepped to the reception and voiced her complaint.

"I want to know why you took down my film?"

The receptionist just stared back at her dispassionately, and pointed to a ticket dispenser. "Take a number and take a seat."

They did so, and parked themselves, ready to unleash all the rage and bluster they had stored up. Meg was angry that she had lost her film and Kay was angry because Meg was angry and it gave her a chance to rant and rave.

Typically, they had a long wait, behind people with general housing complaints and other boring council matters. After an hour or two though, their number came up and they were directed to a nearby office.

Inside sat the slimiest looking official they had ever seen. He was dressed in a shirt and tie and had the least convincing smile Meg had ever seen. As he offered them a seat, Meg noticed that the smile never changed from his face, but his eyes studied the two girls. It made her shiver.

"Now, what's the problem girls?"

"You stole her film!" Kay cried, earning a look from Meg.

"Film?"

"I made a film about The Dead Men." Meg explained. "Winston van Huhn and Craig Vale? They caught zombies?"

The officials grin began to fade as he processed this information. He asked the girls to wait before picking up his phone and dialling through. They sat there as he spoke to someone on the other end, naming both Dead Men and "the whole zombie thing".

There was a silence, before the official put the phone down and turned his attention back to Meg and Kay.

"It seems like your film violated the Council's copyright."

Meg was stunned.

"What does that even mean?" Kay asked.

"My seniors inform me that our logo popped up in your... film. It's a violation of copyright."

"Why?"

"Because you didn't ask our permission."
"Ok, well can I have your permission to show it?" Meg asked.

"In what context?"

"In the context of showing The Dead Men's work catching Moaners."

The official just looked at Meg. "I've no idea what you're talking about."

"The Dead Men! They catch the dead! They put them back!"

The official gave a chuckle and shook his head.

"Your imagination must have ran away with you. Nothing like that exists. Zombies aren't real."

"Yes they are! We saw them! They're in my film."

"Let me say this again little girl," the official said, his tone getting more stern. "Zombies, do not, exist."

Meg felt herself blistering, as Kay just laughed at the official's reaction. She got up, taking Kay with her, and stared at the man in the shirt and tie.

"I'll show you. I'll get them here now."

Meg stormed out with Kay following behind, not seeing the sarcastic wave offered by the official. She decided she would go to van

Huhn and Vale, bring them down there and get the council to let them show their film. It was only fair. It was only right.

But it was not to be.

Vale wasn't home, his Welsh housemate saying he had been picked up an hour or two ago. The same was found at van Huhn's property, where a stranger answered the door and notified them that the van Huhn's had moved, despite their possessions still sitting in place inside.

Suddenly, Meg's fury turned to concern. She began to wonder what she had done by unleashing her film in the public eye. And what she had done to The Dead Men.

Over the next few days Meg got nowhere. No matter how many times she uploaded it, her film was constantly blocked and removed by the powers that be, until her parents sat her down and informed her that they had received a stern letter. They had been told she had been causing trouble and any further attempts by Meg to get her film out there would result in her getting arrested. No matter how much she pleaded, her parents were insistent she let it go.

Unfortunately, despite her early enthusiasm for the fight, Kay began to give up as well. Her energy fading within the first few days.

"Just leave it Meg, it's not *that* worth it surely?"

Meg disagreed. She was inspired to tell the tale of The Dead Men and every attempt to silence her made her more determined to put it out there. But it was a losing battle, and as days turned to weeks she found herself thinking of other projects.

If she was honest, Meg felt a little depressed. After everything she had seen, everything she had learnt, she was now left with nothing but a file taking up space on her hard drive. No-one could ever see the film, and it began to feel like a waste of time. But what made things even worse was she felt like she had ruined peoples lives. Since the film had first gone live, Winston van Huhn and Craig Vale had vanished. Baker said that he no longer saw them down The Patterson Arms, and their properties were sold up and filled with other people. Any record of their existence within the town was stricken off. The Dead Men had become literally that. Dead.

Months passed, and between celebrations of being 18 and moving onto distant universities, Meg and Kay found themselves drifting apart once more. But instead of going their separate ways personally, they remained close, sure that their bond would continue in spite of the distance and varying career paths. There were a lot of emotions at Meg's leaving drinks, helped in part to the sheer amount of legal alcohol they were now quaffing. But at the end of the night, both girls held each other in their arms.

"Meg?" Kay said, tears in her eyes.

"Yeah?"

"I fucking love you."

Meg began to tear up as well.

"I fucking love you too."

And with that, the two girls held each other and cried. Their futures may have been apart but their bond would always be close.

After that, Meg found herself adapting to life as a student, with all the independence it gave her. She began working on new projects with new, exciting people, and found her love of film full of zest.

However, one night, she received an email. There was no obvious name from the user, and the message linked to a Youtube video. Meg clicked and saw a title come up:

ZOMBIE HUNTORZ!!!

Meg watched as blurry footage that had obviously been filmed on a mobile phone offended her eyes. But within the pixelated mess she saw the recognizable shamble of a Moaner. The people recording spoke in excited curses as two men in uniforms approached the figure, shone a light at it and, in the words of the person recording it, 'hooked the fucker!'

Meg sat back in her seat and watched the video finish, the two men in uniform distinguishable by their long hair and beards.

The Dead Men were very much alive.

As always, the author would like to thank all of his family and friends for their help and support in these ramblings. Special merit goes to CM Carter, Graham East, Sam Hussey, Marc Paterson, Michael Williams, Cheryl Wheatley and the Uni Crew.

Oli Jacobs will return in Filmic Cuts 3: Curse of the Ellipsis...